An Imprint of zipper4000 INC
Manchester Center, Vermont 05255

Copyright © 2024 by Ray Mond
All rights reserved, including the right to reproduce this book or portions thereof in any form whatsoever.

First Hardcover edition May 2024

Names: Mond, Ray
Title: CANTGETRITE: to Be Debt-Free, We Must Kill the INTERNET! A More Casual Take on the 9-11 Disaster: Script Book 1 Part South / Ray Mond
Library of Congress Cataloging-in-Publication Data has been applied for CANTGETRITE: to Be Debt-Free, We Must Kill the INTERNET! A More Casual Take on the 9-11 Disaster: Script Book 1 Part South.

Cover, Back and Interior design by Ray Mond
@zipper4000 / Instagram
www.zipper4000.com
www.CantGetRite.com

Library of Congress Control Number: 2024908676

Copyright: 2024
ISBN PAPERBACK: 979-8-9904985-3-2
ISBN HARDCOVER: 979-8-9904985-9-4

MANCHESTER CENTER, VERMONT 05255

Publisher: zipper4000 INC
Manchester Center, Vermont 05255

4

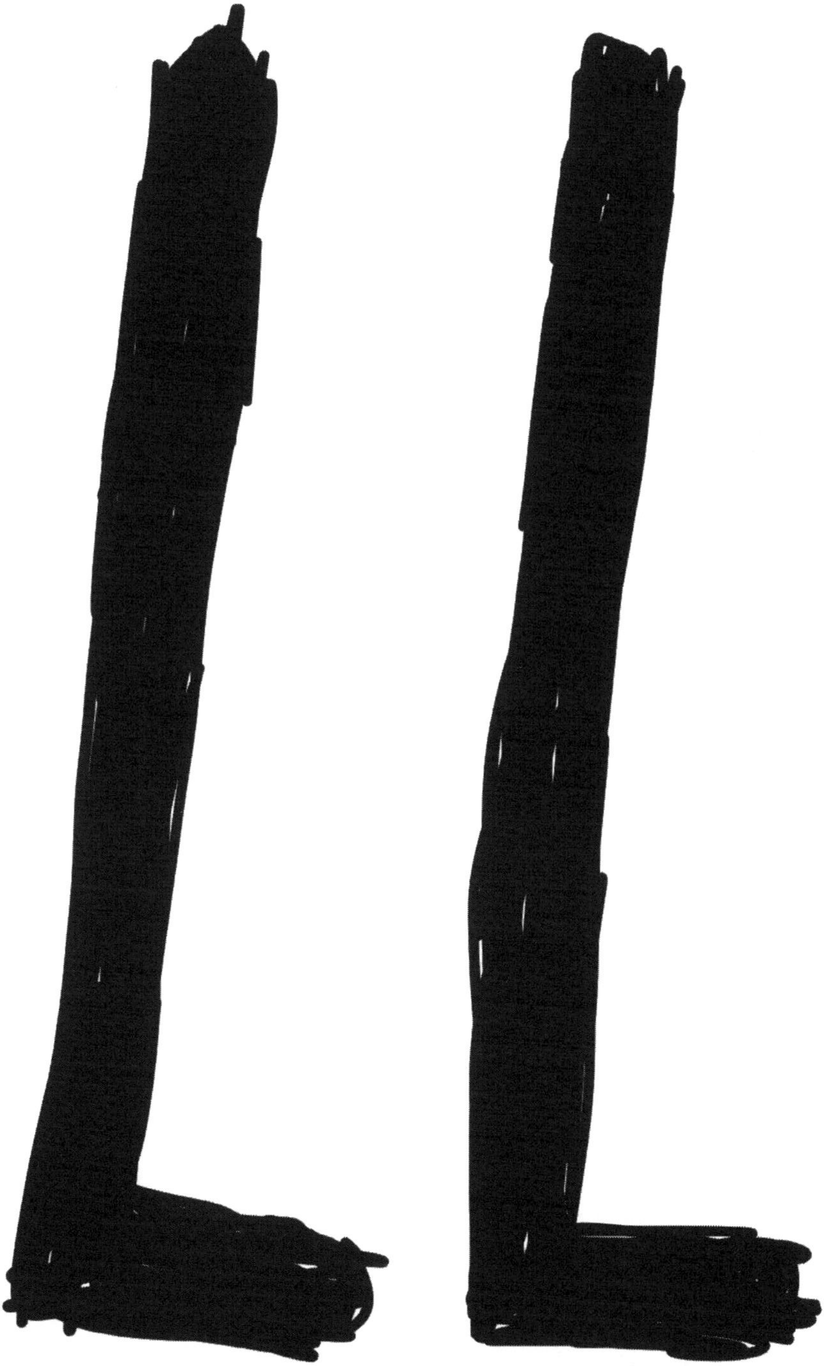

INtc

THE DEVIL, GOD, ALLAH, ODIN, BUDDHA and L. RON HUBBARD walk into a bar......

join da movement

@zipper4000

#KillTheInternet #666 #CantGetRite

                    THE UNIVERSE (O.S.)
What floor, sir?

(SILENCE)

                    THE UNIVERSE (O.S.)(CONT'D)
Mr. Rite?

(SILENCE)

                    THE UNIVERSE (O.S.)(CONT'D)
Cant...

                    CANTGETRITE (O.S.)
              (interrupting)
I'm here to fuck shit up!

Me Dedication

MYSELF! NO ONE ELSE, SAT DOWN AND TYPED THIS SHIT!

                    THE UNIVERSE (O.S.)
No one cares.

ENTER THE BEAST

The Camera zooms all the way up NORTH TOWER

A SHADOW FIGURE appears out of the darkness smoking a vape.

The Camera zooms over to the SOUTH TOWER

THE SHADOW FIGURE disappears back into the darkness after exhaling a large poof of smoke which is masked by the fire pit of smoke inside the building.

The Camera zooms all the way down to the ground.

The Camera PANS UP

EXT. THE TWIN TOWERS - DAY

NBA Finals, music from the visiting team's arena is played.

THE UNIVERSE turns on the THE ANNOUNCER VOICE.

              THE UNIVERSE (V.O.)
        THE DEVIL

THE DEVIL
A pop up on screen show the many names of THE DEVIL:

Lucifer, Satan, Beelzebub, Mephistopheles, Diablo, Old Scratch, Prince of Darkness, The Adversary, The Evil One, The Tempter, The Deceiver, The Fallen One, The Horned One, The Infernal Majesty ,The Wicked One

THE DEVIL kisses towards the CAMERA and walks into the SOUTH TOWER LOBBY.

THE CROWD GOES WILD!

                      THE UNIVERSE (V.O.)
    GOD

GOD
A pop up on screen show the many names of GOD:

The Almighty, The Creator, The Supreme Being, The Divine, The Lord, The Most High, The Holy One, The Eternal, The Alpha and Omega

GOD winks towards the CAMERA and walks into the SOUTH TOWER LOBBY.

THE CROWD GOES WILD!

                      THE UNIVERSE (V.O.)
    ALLAH

ALLAH
A pop up on screen show the many names of ALLAH:

Ar-Rahman (The Compassionate), Ar-Rahim (The Merciful), Al-Malik (The Sovereign), Al-Quddus (The Holy), As-Salam (The Source of Peace), Al-Mu'min (The Guardian of Faith), Al-Muhaymin (The Protector), Al-Aziz (The Mighty), Al-Jabbar (The Compeller), Al-Mutakabbir (The Majestic), Al-Khaliq (The Creator) Al-Bari' (The Evolver), Al-Musawwir (The Fashioner), Al-Ghaffar (The Forgiver), Al-Qahhar (The Subduer)

ALLAH Smiles BIG for the CAMERA and walks into the SOUTH TOWER LOBBY.

THE CROWD GOES WILD!

                    THE UNIVERSE (V.O.)
        ODIN

ODIN
A pop up on screen show the many names of ODIN:

Allfather, Woden, Wotan, Wotanaz, Wodenaz, Wotunn, Wodan, Othin, The Wanderer, The One-eyed, The Raven God, The Hanged God, The Father of Battle, The God of Wisdom

ODIN flexes his biceps towards the CAMERA and walks into the SOUTH TOWER LOBBY.

THE CROWD GOES WILD!

                    THE UNIVERSE (V.O.)
        BUDDHA

BUDDHA
A pop up on screen show the many names of BUDDHA:

Siddhartha Gautama, Shakyamuni Buddha, Gautama Buddha, Tathagata, Sakyamuni, The Enlightened One, The Awakened One, The Blessed One, The Teacher, The Sage of the Sakyas, The Compassionate One, The Great Ascetic, The World-Honored One, The Lion of the Shakya Clan, The Supreme Buddha, The Perfectly Self-Awakened One, The Knower of the World, The King of Dharma, The Master of Nirvana, The Conqueror of Samsara.

BUDDHA Bow to the CAMERA and walks into the SOUTH TOWER LOBBY.

THE CROWD GOES WILD!

THE UNIVERSE (V.O.)
L. RON HUBBARD

L. RON HUBBARD
A pop up on screen show the many names of L. RON HUBBARD:

Lafayette Ronald Hubbard, LRH, RON Hubbard, Elron, The Founder, The Commodore, The Source, Ron the Con

L. RON HUBBARD stops walking and looks up at the pop up that is currently reading "Ron the Con"

L. RON HUBBARD pulls out his rifle and aims it at CHATGPT'S head.

THE CROWD GASPS IN DISBELIEF.

SILENCE!

All we can hear is

CHATGPT, a middle-aged Chinese man, stops typing and quickly deletes the last pop up.

POP UP DISAPPEARS Making a Balloon Sound Noise.

THE CROWD GOES WILD!

L. RON HUBBARD throws gangs signs with a smirk on his face as he walks into the SOUTH TOWER LOBBY.

THE CROWD GOES WILD!

FADE OUT:

SOUTH TOWER LOBBY

                THE UNIVERSE (V.O.)
Welcome to THE TWIN TOWER ARENA brought to you by BITCOIN International.

THE CROWD GOES WILD!

THE DEVIL YELLS...

FADE IN:

INT. SOUTH TOWER LOBBY - DAY

...in GOD'S ear

                GOD
Oh come on man!

THE DEVIL and ODIN high-five one another.

                ODIN
You did it.

                L. RON HUBBARD
He did but, the question is what now?

                BUDDHA
Still a child. Still a child.

                THE DEVIL
Shut the fuck up! Fat thing.

                BUDDHA
Childish.

THE DEVIL Opens up a PORTAL to another UNIVERSE where he grabs the MOON and throws it at CANTGETRITE.

                    BUDDHA
          Get over it.

THE DEVIL Opens up another PORTAL to another
UNIVERSE and squashes CANTGETRITE with just his
INDEX FINGER.

                    ALLAH
          Let him. No one can stop him and I bet it feels so
          good.

THE DEVIL continues to open up multiple PORTALS to other
UNIVERSES just to KILL ANOTHER CANTGETRITE

                    ALLAH (O.S.)
          Dam that bad eh.

THE DEVIL kills another CANTGETRITE

                    GOD
          Are you seriously going to kill everyone of them?

                    THE DEVIL
          Yes.

                    GOD
          That's going to take awhile and we're going to be
          late.

THE DEVIL squashes another CANTGETRITE from another
UNKNOWN UNIVERSE that is viewed by an open portal that
THE DEVIL opens.

THE DEVIL'S CELLPHONE RINGS.

FACETIME - THE DEVIL'S PHONE

> KAREN
>
> I found him!

> THE DEVIL
>
> Are you certain?

> KAREN
>
> Don't fucking test me, I took the day off and I used up my precision time for something that can easily done by you but, you are a lazy piece of shit. Don't fucking test me you prick! You promised! You need to do your...

THE DEVIL hits the MUTE BUTTON.

THE DEVIL just nods to Karen who is continuing to verbal rant with out the the knowledge of being muted.

THE DEVIL hits the MUTE BUTTON.

> THE DEVIL
>
> Send me the location.

> KAREN
>
> You better squash that little fucker for touc...

THE DEVIL hits the MUTE BUTTON again.

Karen finally finishes her rants.

THE DEVIL hits the MUTE BUTTON again.

> KAREN
>
> Here's the coordinates.

> THE DEVIL
>
> Oh happy day. You did well Karen.

Karen continues to RANT as THE DEVIL hangs up the phone.

BACK TO SCENE

USPS POSTAL MAN appears him THE DEVIL'S FACE

                    USPS POSTAL MAN
        Have a package for GODS INC.

THE DEVIL'S POV

                    THE DEVIL (O.S.)
     Da fuck man, don't you even knock?

THE PACKAGE is from THE INTERNET and the return address reads: "#1 PENTHOUSE, NORTH TOWER

                    THE DEVIL
        Guys... I Have an idea.

GOD, BUDDHA, ALLAH, ODIN, and L. RON HUBBARD stop in their tracks.

BUDDHA is the only one shaking his head.

THE DEVIL'S PHONE RINGS

THE DEVIL'S POV

Karen is calling.

THE DEVIL clicks on IGNORE and TURNS OFF HIS CELLPHONE.

FADE TO WHITE

FLOOR 1

KILL YOURSELF!

"KILL YOURSELF" FLASHES 16 TIMES ON SCREEN FOR 3:17 SECONDS

GOVERNMENT COMPUTER SOFTWARE STARTS LOADING

THE INTERNET, a man dressed causal, walks up to the CAMERA and pulls out a mic from his back pocket.

>   THE INTERNET
> Pshhhkkkkkkrrrrrkakingkakingkakingtshchchchchchch chch*ding*ding*ding*

>   THE INTERNET
> Welcome to THE INTERNET!

>   THE DEVIL (O.S.)
> ...The Devil is ready to play boys. Place your bets. Place your bets. Place your bets! It's time to place your bets HE/SHE/IT losers!

THE INTERNET extends his arms like a GOD as he welcomes everyone into the ethernet.

THE INTERNET dissolves into the world wide web.

Computer Cursor quickly types on the screen.

CANTGETRITE: "To Be Debt-Free, We Must Kill THE INTERNET!"...

THE CURSOR continues to blink

COMPUTER SOFTWARE CRASHES

                CANTGETRITE (V.O.)
Funny thing happened to me on the way to the Twin Towers…

                                      SMASH CUT TO:

INT. NORTH TWIN TOWERS - NIGHT

FADE TO:

SMOKE, FIRE, EXPLOSIONS, AND DOZENS OF SCIENTISTS ARE SCREAMING

                CANTGETRITE (V.O.)
On 9-11.

A FIREBALL EXPLOSION ruptures behind

CANTGETRITE, black 46, FREDDY ROACH, white 46, and WET~RICE Asian 46, the only one holding a RICE COOKER and wearing a FACE MASK, runs down a flight of steel stairs and all while dodging HUNDREDS OF SCIENTIST, wearing lab coats.

                FREDDY ROACH
We should have taken the elevators!

A BURNING ELEVATOR with SCREAMING SCIENTISTS inside zips past Freddy, WET~RICE, and CantGetRite, crashing out of the 74th Floor. WET~RICE'S eyes widen with a THICK ASIAN ACCENT.

                WET~RICE
Wow, that look fun!

Freddy looks at WET~RICE and wonders what's wrong with her.

CANTGETRITE
I'd rather take the stairs!

CANTGETRITE - POV

NORTH AND SOUTH TWIN TOWERS ARE ON FIRE

ANOTHER BURNING ELEVATOR crashes onto the GROUND with 6 DEAD SCIENTIST popping out of the door on impact.

INT. NORTH TWIN TOWERS - NIGHT

GUST OF WIND blows everyone toward the broken windows.

A FEW SCIENTIST falls out of the 74th floor windows.

FREDDY - POV

WET~RICE drops her rice-cooker, falling out the window and screaming in pure orgasmic excitement.

Freddy grabs a rope, ties it to the building's exposed frame, and wraps it around his waist, all while jumping out the window in attempt to save WET~RICE.

WET~RICE - POV

Falling to certain death, WET~RICE focuses on grabbing her rice-cooker in mid-air.

RICE COOKER - POV - CONTINUOUS

WET~RICE gleaming in excitement

                WET~RICE
  My rice!

CUT TO:

MID-AIR - CONTINUOUS

Freddy grabs WET~RICE's hand as WET~RICE finally grabs onto her RICE-COOKER. She holds onto it.

INT. NORTH TWIN TOWERS - CONTINUOUS

The rope gets untied

CantGetRite jumps onto the runaway rope.

CantGetRite is struggling to pull everyone up.

76th FLOOR WINDOW

A YOUNG MAN appears out the burning window, making eye contact with the gang as he looks down 76 stories.

YOUNG MAN pulls out an UMBRELLA and OPENS IT.

                CANTGETRITE
       (yelling towards The Young MAN)
  It not going to work!

                WET~RICE
  Do it!

Young Man jumps and floats in the air for half a second.

                FREDDY ROACH
  Well, I be…

Young Man's umbrella immediately breaks and free falls 76 stories to the ground.

WET~RICE
(Towards Young Man)
Stupid Pierre Salinger.

YOUNG MAN hits the ground hard!

THE GROUND is covered with hundreds of SCIENTIST that are dead on the GROUND.

CantGetRite continues to struggle to pull up Freddy and WET~RICE.

THE GANG'S - POV

74 stories to the ground, THE TWIN TOWERS continue to burn intensely.

A COUPLE OF SCIENTISTS jump out of the burning building, falling to death.

CantGetRite continues to struggle as the weight of Freddy and WET~RICE start to drag CantGetRite slowly toward the edge of the window's structure.

INT. NORTH TWIN TOWERS - NIGHT

    FREDDY ROACH
   (screaming)
 I don't want to die, Cant!

CantGetRite slowly starts pulling the rope up.

    CANTGETRITE (V.O.)
 You can do this! You can do this!

CantGetRite exerts all his energy pulling the rope.

                    CANTGETRITE
                    (To himself)
            You can do this! You can do this!

The rope starts to tear apart his palms.

                    CantGETRITE
                    (yelling to himself)
                Come on Can! Come on!

CantGetRite pulls up Freddy and WET~RICE.

Freddy quickly hugs and kisses an exhausted CantGetRite.

                    FREDDY ROACH
        Oh my god, I thought I was going to die! Oh my god!
        Never thought I be happy to kiss a black man!

CantGetRite, Freddy, and WET~RICE sit on the edge of the window, exhausted.

WET~RICE screams out like a banshee in excitement.

                    WET~RICE
                What a rush!

CantGetRite and Freddy stare at WET~RICE.

Everything around them is on fire while CantGetRite bandages' his bleeding palms.

SERIES OF SHOTS

A) CantGetRite pulls out his vape pen and vapes.

B) CantGetRite passes the vape pen.

CANTGETRITE
Smoke it. It'll help calm you down when everything around you is crumbling.

C) Freddy vapes and immediately coughs.

D) Freddy passes the vape pen to WET~RICE. She pulls down her mask to vape. WET~RICE gives the vape pen back to CantGetRite.

E) CantGetRite shakes the vape pen and tosses it out of the NORTH TWIN TOWER'S 74th-floor broken window.

BITCOIN NOTIFICATION SOUND

Freddy and WET~RICE check their phones.

BITCOIN
Bitcoin is up today!

CantGetRite shakes his head as he looks at both WET~RICE and FREDDY toast each other using their cellphones.

We see a lone SCIENTIST holding onto dear life.

LONE SCIENTIST
Bitcoin is up?

WET~RICE
It sure is.

The LONE SCIENTIST pulls out his cellphone to check his notifications only to realize that he was currently holding onto dear life with the only free hand he had.

The LONE SCIENTIST falls 70+ stories to the ground.

THE GANG'S POV

THE SOUTH TOWER CRASHES TO THE GROUND

                        CANTGETRITE
                 (Whispering to himself)
      This was a very very very bad idea.

                      THE UNIVERSE (O.S.)
                 (whispers)
      No one gives a flyin fuck!

The SOUND of the LONE SCIENTIST hits the ground.

LONE SCIENTIST'S CELLPHONE.

BITCOIN IS UP!

A MESSAGE NOTIFICATION POPS ON THE SCREEN.

FLOOR 2

UNIVERSE GROUP TEXT

CU - CANTGETRITE'S EYES

Looking at the READER, which is YOU... not ME. Well, that's confusing isn't it?

    THE UNIVERSE (O.S.)
What's real?

CantGetRite looks at THE UNIVERSES.

    THE UNIVERSE (O.S.)
What really is... real?

Billions of stars, flickering like a light show that would give anyone an epileptic seizures just by staring at it for more than 6 seconds.

    THE UNIVERSE (V.O.)
If all your senses are lying than what do you believe when even your eyes have a story of their own.

CantGetRite's pupils dilate and start forming into a GALAXY.

    THE UNIVERSE (V.O.)
Believe what you want to believe.

    CANTGETRITE
Oh for fuck sakes.

    THE UNIVERSE (V.O.)
   (Whispering)
Just be happy, that you aren't blind.

FADE TO BLACK

> BUDDHA (O.S.)
> This isn't the Buddha way.

FADE TO WHITE

THE SCREEN LOOKS LIKE A CELLPHONE DISPLAY

> THE DEVIL (O.S.)
> Oh, shut the fuck up you fat fuck!

> GOD
> Stop playin' and lets get down to business.

> THE DEVIL
> Playin' is my business.

WIFI ICON APPEARS ON THE TOP RIGHT CORNER

GROUP TEXT

>ODIN (TEXT)
>I, Odin, is down to play. What about you, Mr. L. Ron Hubbard?

>L. RON HUBBARD (TEXT)
>It's only money. What do you say, Allah?

SUPER: CANTGETRITE V THE INTERNET: THE BATTLE TO BE GODS

>ALLAH (TEXT)
>Assalamulaikum... the hell with it! #MeToo. What about you, my brother?

SUPER: A more casual take on the 9-11 disaster

>GOD (TEXT)
>Jesus Christ man!...Watch me get blamed for this all this bullshit!

SUPER: YESTERDAY

>BUDDHA (TEXT)
>Emoji rolling eyes.

>THE DEVIL (TEXT)
>All bets are in!

>ODIN (TEXT)
>Odin asks, what about Buddha?

Buddha thumbs up Odin's message.

                    THE DEVIL (TEXT)
     He. She. It. What ever fuck pronoun Buddha is. It has missed the boat? This is defiantly one of my best ideas yet!

THE DEVIL clicks "HAHA" on his message.

FUCK GOD! FUCK ALLAH! FUCK THE DEVIL! FUCK ODIN! FUCK BUDDHA! FUCK L. RON HUBBARD! FUCK YO BITCH!

Floor 3

FUCK YOUR FAITH!

INT. CANTGETRITE'S BEDROOM - MORNING

          THE UNIVERSE (V.O.)
There is no way.
    (beat)
You are in the way.

SUPER: PRESENT DAY

CantGetRite wakes up annoyed, grabs a cup of water, and drinks it while looking straight at the CAMERA and BREAKING THE 4TH WALL.

             CANTGETRITE
Missed the boat, YOLO, don't do anything for a buck, living the dream. You know all those stupid catchphrases or what ever you want to call them to make you feel like you're saying something important when, in fact...

CantGetRite takes a hit off his weed bong.

             CANTGETRITE
Wake and bake muthafucka. Ok, where was I?...

CantGetRite takes another hit of his bong.

             CANTGETRITE
Oh that's right. You ain't said shit! Fuck your noise and fuck you. Yeah I have issues. We all do. But, nothing like me. But...

CantGetRite continues to smoke.

                              CANTGETRITE
                  My favorite. Oh gawd!
                        (mocking an old man)
                  You got to pay your dues, kid!
                        (Porky Pig's voice)
                  What dues? What in the fuck... I say, what in the
                  fuck. Dues?

CantGetRite stands on his bed in one swoop motion as a demon-possessed.

CantGetRite shakes his head ever so slightly.

                                                    SMASH CUT TO:

INT. ST. RAYMOND'S BAPTIST CHURCH - CONTINUOUS

MC HAMMER SONG "PRAY" plays

Confetti and balloons appear from the sky.

TWO 6-YEAR-OLD ALTER BOYS rip off CantGetRite's PJ, exposing a GQ TAN SUIT.

A CHOIR APPEARS behind CantGetRite.

                              CANTGETRITE
                  This is one of many reasons I can't make bread.

A CAMERA MAN APPEARS with a FILM PRODUCTION CREW NEARBY.

SERIES OF SHOTS

A) THE DEVIL is eating popcorn and enjoying the show.

B) GOD counting the money from the donations basket while drinking wine and eating crackers

C) Allah is praying while responding to his INSTAHOES account.

D) Odin is passed out sleeping.

E) L.RON HUBBARD is reading the Entertainment News on his phone.

F) Buddha is meditating.

Unknown forces are forcing CantGetRite to dance with the CHOIR, who are singing along with CantGetRite.

CantGetRite dances like a pro while not staring at THE DEVIL intensely.

THE DEVIL blows a kiss towards CantGetRite, acknowledging him.

SERIES OF FLASHBACK

CantGetRite continues to fight the controlling forces that is making him break dance yet knows it's futile.

     CANTGETRITE
    (Dancing)
  All bets are off!

A) CantGetRite riding on top of NOAH'S ARK towards the end of Earth.

B) GERMAN WAR SOLIDER points a gun at CantGetRite's head.

C) SOUTH TOWER crashing onto CantGetRite.

D) CantGetRite trying to break free from the GODS' CONTROL while doing the splits like JAMES BROWN.

> CANTGETRITE (O.S.)
> I just can't.

E) CantGetRite is given back control of his body.

F) THE CHOIR fades into the distance.

G) CantGetRite shakes his head while taking a deep breath.

CANTGETRITE LOOKS AT THE CAMERA

> CANTGETRITE
> (notices his hands are trembling)
> I can't. I've had it and about to lose my shit. This is an on going issue and I'm just ready to go postal on someone, and not give a fuck.

THE DEVIL stands up and extends his arms out, waiting for CantGetRite to say something he already knows what he's about to hear.

CantGetRite and THE DEVIL'S eyes lock.

THE DEVIL smiles slowly and enjoys every Sybille out of CantGetRite's mouth.

> CANTGETRITE
> (Towards THE DEVIL)
> Fuck you!

THE DEVIL'S full smile appears as he takes a bite out of a HUGE POPCORN in the shape of an APPLE.

                        CANTGETRITE
                        (Towards GOD)
    Fuck you!

GOD stops counting money to look up.

                        CANTGETRITE
                        (Towards Allah)
    Fuck you!

Allah stops praying, flips the middle finger to CantGetRite, and continues to pray.

                        CANTGETRITE
                        (Towards Odin)
    Fuck you!

ODIN is drooling while he's still in a deep sleep.

                        CANTGETRITE
                        (Towards L.RON HUBBARD)
    Fuck you!...

L.RON HUBBARD quickly looks up and returns to his Hollywood News.

CantGetRite looks at BUDDHA, who opens up one eye, sensing CantGetRite about to talk to him.

                        CANTGETRITE
                        (Towards Buddha)
    ...And fuck you too!

Buddha takes a deep breath and stares back quietly.

THE TWO 6-YEAR-OLD ALTER BOYS return to rip CantGetRite into two pieces right before CantGetRite slaps both boys in the ass as he makes the same squealing noise, MICHEAL JACKSON does during singing.

"They Don't Care About Us by Michael Jackson" plays

Both ALTER BOYS are covered in BLOOD. One is holding CantGetRite's right side of his flesh, bones, and guts while the other ALTER BOY is hold the left side of his flesh, bones and, heart.

BLOOD EVERYWHERE

Fireworks explode in the air, confetti falls from the ceiling and, balloons appear out of nowhere.

A SINGULAR BRIGHT LIGHT emerges out of CantGetRite's body.

THE SINGULAR BRIGHT LIGHT expands and contracts.

THE DEVIL, GOD, ALLAH, BUDDHA, and L. RON HUBBARD stand up and applaud.

THE BRIGHT LIGHT blankets the Church.

CantGetRite Disappears.

                      THE DEVIL
              (Putting on sunglasses)
  Looks like someone woke up on the wrong side of the bed again.

THE DEVIL snaps his fingers, bring back to life MICHEAL JACKSON.

Micheal Jackson squeals.

THE DEVIL snaps his fingers agains, causing Michel Jackson to disappear.

Micheal Jackson squeals again.

                                        FADE TO WHITE:

APPLAUSES CONTINUES.

FLOOR 4

FEDERAL ROBOT

FADE IN:

EXT. FEDERAL COBALT MINING FACILITY - DAY

SUPER: FEDERAL COBALT MINING FACILITY - 222.2 Miles from Central Newer Oak City

We hear ODIN waking up.

> ODIN (O.S.)
> What happened?

FEDERAL ROBOT mining agent kicks ODIN, who is laying on the Cobalt dirt floor.

> FEDERAL ROBOT
> You slepted on the job again, slave!
> (kicking ODIN again)
> Get up and start mining!

Federal Robot kicks ODIN once more as it walks away.

AERIAL VIEW

Over 6000 MEN, WOMEN, and CHILDREN are jammed in together, mining Colbart on the West side of the facility.

We zoom over the crowded miners and into the open windows of

INT. FEDERAL MINING OFFICE - CONTINUES

MOSES, 99, Federal Worker sitting behind his desk tapping the ENTER KEY repeatably on his DESKTOP COMPUTER.

The computer is frozen on a NETFLIX SCREEN, and we see only 3 Movie choices.

Moses hits the enter key harder each time, grabs the keyboard, and is about to hit the monitor with the keyboard.

                MOSES
    God dam slooo…

In Burst, FEDERAL ROBOT, looks exactly how you imagine a FEDERAL ROBOT looks like. Exposed dirty steel parts and a machine-like face.

                FEDERAL ROBOT
    Moses no!

               MOSES (CONT'D)
    Oooow IN…

Moses caught himself.

                FEDERAL ROBOT
    Don't scare me like that.

                MOSES
    Still find it hard to believe you Robots got feelings.

                FEDERAL ROBOT
    We do, and under all this metal tough external, I'm sensitive; you should know that by now. I don't like to be called a Robot. I'm a Federal Agent for Section 76. I'm deeply concerned with your mental health Moses. Almost sounds like you have a split

personality at times. My therapist always starts out by asking. What's really going on, Moses?

           MOSES
You wouldn't understand; you couldn't

           FEDERAL ROBOT
It's not about my understanding. It's about your understanding of my understanding and not the other way around.

           MOSES
Look at this! Just look at it!

Moses points at his computer monitor.

           MOSES
We just have three channels. Not one...not two but three channels. GNN Channel, DJ JILL.MP3 channel and, Netflix. The only movie channel we got and what do they give us? Just three movies a year, and what do we get? All apocalypse genera with the same formula. A man with amnesia wakes up in new world.

CU - MOSES'S COMPUTER

We see 3 movie posters.

           MOSES
Dinosaurs kill the planet!

TOMMY CRUISE is riding a Dinosaurs Rex while eating Ice Cream.

           MOSES
Astroid kills the planet!

TOMMY CRUISE is riding a spaceship while eating Ice Cream.

          MOSES
And Zombies Kills the plant!

TOMMY CRUISE is a ZOMBIE while eating Ice Cream.

          MOSES
And it's always with the same dam actor! The thespian GOD himself.

          FEDERAL ROBOT (O.S.)
Who?

          MOSES
He is considered The Thespian God.

          THE DEVIL
And who's the one that gave him that title?

SILENCE

INT. UNIVERSE - UNKNOWN

          BUDDHA
That would be me.

          THE DEVIL
So essentially you are to no longer to give out GOD titles effective immediately.

          BUDDHA
I can say the same thing about you.

          THE DEVIL
Me? Me?.. You little fat fuck.

                    ODIN
Well didn't you give Karen a title?

                    GOD
Oh that complainer has a GOD title?

                    THE DEVIL
Yes.

                    ALLAH
Why!
          (beat)
No seriously why?
          (beat)
Why!

INT. FEDERAL MINING OFFICE - CONTINUES

Moses points and then continues to tap at his computer monitor as The Federal Robot sees TOMMY CRUISE riding an Astroid.

                    MOSES
Him! Him!

                    FEDERAL ROBOT
Oh, I love him!
          (beat)
But, really Moses. What's going on. Talking about it makes you know that the problem is real and can be fixed. The problem is real and I can help you fix it.

                    MOSES
No shit the problem is real. Everyday it's the same thing. Day in and Day out. I'm ok. You aren't my therapist.

FEDERAL ROBOT
I understand but, I can be for an extra $2.99 a month subscription to my channel?

MOSES
Wait! You got your own channel?

Floor 5

MOSES

Federal Robot pulls out a BOX shaped like a SLICE OF CAKE

> FEDERAL ROBOT
> I know why you have the blues lately. Happy Birthday Moses.

Moses is pissed but, takes a deep breathe knowing that he is upset with a Robot that identifies as a human.

> MOSES
> Thanks but, that's not the reason why I have been off these weeks and I don't want to talk about it. Talking about it does nothing. Nothing for me!

> FEDERAL ROBOT
> It's ok, I understand.

> MOSES
> Ha! You understand.

> FEDERAL ROBOT
> And how do you feel?

> MOSES
> I ain't going to tell you.

> FEDERAL ROBOT
> You're in control. It's up to you.

> MOSES
> And guess what!

FEDERAL ROBOT
Do tell.

MOSES
Mind your business.

FEDERAL ROBOT
I'm always available when you're ready to open up.

MOSES
I just woke up to find Alexa in my bed with her legs spread out.

FEDERAL ROBOT
THE INTERNET'S girl?

MOSES
It's not my fault. And THE INTERNET gave me leanacy but, I just fuck it up every year. Every fucking year it's the same dam thing. I fucking swear I can't do it again.

FEDERAL ROBOT
I understand.

MOSES
No. No you don't. You don't have a dick!

FEDERAL ROBOT
Help me understand.

MOSES
I have the power to part things like no one's business. It's not my fault that I bumped into SIRI at a BITCOIN convention in Tokyo where I was celebrating my 18th birthday.

INT. TOKYO CONVENTION CENTER - NIGHT

17 year old MOSES looks at his cellphone and a notification appears. "1 hour til your 18th birthday"

      FEDERAL ROBOT
What a way to celebrated your 18th.

      MOSES
Waking up to Siri in bed and she's right there begging you to fuck her. The closer she got to me, the more her legs spread apart for me. It was then I found out about the powers of The Moses.

      FEDERAL ROBOT
Did you just call yourself in the 3rd person...

      MOSES
Yes because every year it happens. And after all these years. This might be the year for me. I'm so happy that I can't get it up no more. The stipulation of the agreement from the contract when I was charged for having intercourse with THE INTERNET'S girl which is a federal offensive rule which by luck of the draw I barely turned 18 which instead of life sentence. I was charged for one year to service at Colbart factory of the government choice after which if I did the crime again, I will only get one year.

      FEDERAL ROBOT
So what's the problem. Why couldn't you just avoid contact?

      MOSES
Yeah seems easy buddy right?

      FEDERAL ROBOT
I didn't mean to hurt your feelings.

MOSES
You didn't. I'm just being an asshole because she just appears in my bed the night of my birthday, you dumb fuck iron piece of... and my powers are always strong in spreading her legs apart.

FEDERAL ROBOT
Seems like you will be charged again. You need to lay off the drugs because you are having multiple conversation and it all leads no where.

MOSES
Seems that way but, not this time. I can't get it up no more. Ha ha ha ha. Fuck THE INTERNET and his hoes. This weenie no longer in combat mode.
    (beat)
What were we talking about?

Moses is laughing so hard that the workers can hear him outside.

MOSES
(Smiling)
I can't get it up no more!

THE WORKERS starting to chant.

Moses starts to sing, I can't get it up no more until he releases it's not good to sing.

THE WORKERS give out a weak clap.

Moses starts crying.

MOSES
And why are we stopping!

All the workers continue to mine.

FEDERAL ROBOT
It's ok Moses. It's going to be ok.

MOSES
Why am I so happy that my dick doesn't work?

FEDERAL ROBOT
You're old.

MOSES
Old?

Federal Robot pops out a mirror and Moses sees a very old person looking back at him.

MOSES
Holy split balls! I'm old.

FLOOR 6

YOUNG COCKROACH

KNOCK AT THE DOOR

> FEDERAL ROBOT
> Your appointment is here and on time.

Moses stops laughing and looks at the documents on his desk.

> MOSES
> They are just getting younger and younger each year.

MOSES looks at the MIRROR to Adjust his tie and hair. MOSES'S mirror reflects him a little younger, MOSES, 79

YOUNG FREDDY ROACH 26 walks in.

> MOSES
> Well, look at you, young and already having the best pathetic life eva'.

FEDERAL ROBOT, looking new, hands Moses Freddy's paperwork.

> MOSES
> Looks like the judge threw the book at you!

FLASHBACK

INT. FEDERAL COURT - DAY

> JUDGE
> It looks like you are pleading the court for some leniency because...

The JUDGE is skimming through all of FREDDY ROACH'S hospital papers.

> JUDGE
> Were you in a coma for 6 years?

FREDDY ROACH, 26 stands up.

> FREDDY ROACH
> Yes, your Honor.

> JUDGE
> I can understand your frustration.

> FREDDY ROACH
> Thank you, your Honor...

> JUDGE
> (Interrupting)
> Hold on. I'm getting a message.
> (beat)
> THE INTERNET accepts your plea and will reduce your time from 20 years to 6 years.

> FREDDY ROACH
> All just for saying, THE INTERNET sucks, and it's slow?!

> JUDGE
> I don't care if you were born yesterday or can't read. You are hear by charged 6 counts of Treason and threats to overcome THE INTERNET. Your Bitcoin wallet is now the property of the state.

> FREDDY ROACH
> Wait!...THE INTERNET is a real person?

END OF FLASHBACK

INT. MOSES APARTMENT - NIGHT

Moses, 99, unpacks, undresses and heads to the shower.

> GOVERNMENT JUDGE (O.S.)
> The Government of Flat Earth Section code 6 dash 67823 that Moses has completed his 1 year at Federal Mining sector 8 for the crime 1.pino Code dash 2 of section 1a that under no circumstances one will have sexual relationship with THE INTERNET'S girl Siri. Failure will result in immediate detention in Federal Mining Sector 8 for the maximum in the case of Moses will be one calendar year starting the following hour.

Moses gets out of the shower and puts on a towel.

> MOSES
> Oh I missed a powerful shower. Just need some music and a wonderful night sleep on this comfortable bed. Nothing can stop me now.

Moses starts singing.

> MOSES
> Going to need some jazz music tonight.

Moses notices his new cellphone that he just unpacked.

> MOSES
> Hey Siri...

Moses immediately shows regret in his face as he forgot to not mentioned Siri.

SIRI POPS in Moses' bed.

SIRI in a teddy crawls over to Moses.

> SIRI
> Hi daddy!

> MOSES
> Please Siri... not this time. All I wanted was a little bit of jazz music. Please

SIRI now has her legs spread over Moses' body.

> MOSES
> Please. Please... I'm too old for this shit.

> SIRI
> Ok.

Moses shocked to hear SIRI agree.

> MOSES
> Ok?

JAZZ MUSIC is filling the apartment.

> SIRI
> Ok. I'm playing your playlist that you wanted me to play for you babe.

> MOSES
> How the hell am I getting an erection? This isn't possible.

SIRI'S eyes light up as she fills Moses poking her.

> SIRI
> Oh Moses! You do love me!

MOSES
There's no way.
(beat)
No no no no no no no. There's no fucking way.

SIRI
When there's fucking, there's a way.
(beat)
And with you daddy. There's always a way.

Moses looks like he wants to cry but, can't.

SIRI
Remember the complimentary cup of water that was given to you after leaving the courtroom?

MOSES - FLASHBACK

Moses looks up at the Judge and takes a deep breathe.

MOSES
Thank you your honor. I understand what I did wrong and will not do it again.

FEDERAL JUDGE
You're looking a little parched.

Moses chuckles a bit.

MOSES
It's all those months working in a Colbart mining field. My throat been giving me issues.

FEDERAL JUDGE
Have some complimentary ice cold water straight from the Government's tap. It's guarantee to help with that, I just worked 100 hours a week and I have nothing to show for it feeling.

The Bailiff, a woman wearing a mask, hands Moses a cup of water.

      BAILIFF
  It's mountain water that will give you a spring feel.

Moses drinks it.

         END OF
         FLASHBACK

INT. MOSES APARTMENT - NIGHT

SIRI has her legs wrapped around Moses.

      SIRI
  That spring water sure made you all sprung up for
  me love.

SIRI starts to spread her legs even wider.

      SIRI
  Oh Moses.
    (beat)
  Hey JILL.MP3

JILL.MP3 appears as a hologram on Moses' apartment ceiling.

      JILL.MP3
  Hi Moses.

      MOSES
  Hey Jill.

      SIRI
  Can you play Jazz remixes for my lover.

MOSES
Please no.

JILL.MP3
Can I stream it this time?

SIRI
Oh yes!

MOSES
Oh no.

JILL.MP3 starts DJing in her fame two piece pink bikini while streaming.

JILL.MP3
This is JILL.MP3 Live in the mix with Moses and Siri ready for some action so hot that it won't be played for till another year. Get your headsets on, volume on up and get ready to bounce.

SIRI
Oh I'll be bouncing on daddy for sure.

MOSES
(shaking his head)
Oh fuck me.

SIRI
Oh daddy!

MOSES - POV

Moses looks up to the MIRROR CEILING to see

JILL.MP3 DJing LIVE while SIRI is riding him.

INT. FEDERAL MINING OFFICE - continuous

Moses looks at his mirror again and sees himself in the present time as an old 99-year-old man.

>   MOSES
>   (to himself)
> Fuck!

>   MOSES
> So tell me…

Old dirty looking Federal Robot hands Moses a tablet.

>   MOSES
> Fred.

FRED, 26-year-old Hispanic, quietly looks back at Moses.

>   MOSES
> Follow me.

>   FEDERAL ROBOT
> Oh and happy be-lated birthday!

Moses slams the door in the Federal Robot's face.

>   MOSES
> Fuck you!

Floor 7

THE FINGER

EXT. FEDERAL COBALT MINING FACILITY - CONTINUOUS

Moses walks into the mining field. 6000 miners part ways as Moses walks through.

>MOSES
>Your files say that you're a paid actor?

>FRED
>Thespian before my accident.

>MOSES
>Well, you better act like you enjoy mining Cobalt because I don't care if you got an Emmy or an Oscar. You're responsible for mining Cobalt in your 16-hour shift schedule. Do you understand!

One MINER is jumping the fence and running.

>MINER (O.S.)
>We got a runner!

Moses looks at the MINER that is on the run.

>MOSES
>This is a perfect example.

ALL THE MINORS are starting to cheer for the lone Miner that is attempting to run.

MOSES
Now look at this idiot for example. If you can escape, dodge THE FINGER and travel 222 without getting the finger, then consider yourself free. Free at last. You will be home free.

FRED
The Finger? Free?

A HUGE FINGER appears from the sky.

MINER successfully escapes the facility while dodging 2 HUGE FINGERS from the sky.

All 6000 Miner, cheer on a fellow Miner.

MOSES
Now all he has to do is dodge The Finger for the next 222 miles, and he is home free.

FRED
And what happens if he doesn't?

All 6000 Miners start chanting!

The Chanting gets louder and louder each and every time He dodges THE FINGER from the SKY.

FRED
Looks like he's going to make it.

MOSES
Give it a sec.

The MINER continues to dodge multiple BIG FINGERS but is visibly tired.

ONE MINER gives the sky THE MIDDLE FINGER

FINGER from the sky smashes THE MINER.

PHONE SOUND NOTIFICATION - DING! DING! DING!

INT. PHIL'S APARTMENT

PHIL is tapping his CELLPHONE fast.

BITCOIN SOUND NOTIFICATION

PHIL'S CELLPHONE

      BITCOIN
Congratulations Phil! You just acquired one bitcoin!

ONE BITCOIN transfers into Phil's GOVERNMENT ACCOUNT

Phil jumps up knocking THE HOOKER that was sucking his cock to the ground.

Phil reaches to the stars in excitement as his pants completely fall to the ground.

          BACK TO SCENE

EXT. FEDERAL COBALT MINING FACILITY - CONTINUOUS

      MOSES
  Three. Two. One.
    (beat)

ANOTHER HUGE FINGER appears out of the sky, squashing the ANOTHER MINER to death.

Blood and guts are all over.

MOSES does a stupid KUN FU POSE.

> MOSES
> Death by finger.

PHONE SOUND NOTIFICATION - DING! DING! DING!

INT. CINDY'S APARTMENT - DAY

BITCOIN SOUND NOTIFICATION

CINDY'S CELLPHONE

> BITCOIN
> Congratulations Cindy! You just acquired one bitcoin!

ONE BITCOIN transfers into Cindy's GOVERNMENT ACCOUNT

CINDY, a 6-year old child is tapping hard and quickly on her cellphone screen.

CINDY - POV

CELLPHONE

THE FINGER APP

> HUE.USA.GOV-REPORTER (O.S.)
> What is THE FINGER APP? And why is it important to our society?

THE INTERNET appears on THE FINGER APP

> THE INTERNET
> THE FINGER APP or how I like to call it. A hand out to the citizens of flat earth. With the finger app you can provide for you and your family with a simple.

THE INTERNET taps his cellphone.

                THE INTERNET
It's that easy. You will receive a notification that the Government.

POTUS ICE CREAM appears on the screen.

                POTUS ICE CREAM
I'll take it from here sunshine.

You can tell that THE INTERNET and POTUS ICE CREAM dispise one another yet are making a front for the flat earth.

POTUS ICE CREAM pulls out his cellphone.

                POTUS ICE CREAM
It's easy folks. Notification will pop on the screen.

                MOSES (O.S.)
We got a runner!

INT. FEDERAL COBALT MINING FACILITY

A MINOR is frantically running away from the facility.

THE CROWD GOES WILD!

EVERYONE STARTS TO CHANT!

                POTUS ICE CREAM (O.S.)
The Government is afraid to admit that we are running low on energy and with the state of cellphone art technology and a tap of the phone, you can transfer mega walts of energy to our sector.

                THE INTERNET (O.S.)
I see that the Government is in need of help!

NOTIFICATION POPS ON SCREEN

THE MINOR has succeed in running out of the facility and is headed to the open road.

THE FINGER APP

              THE INTERNET
Tapping is helpful.

            POTUS ICE CREAM
We can agree on one thing.

              THE INTERNET
The first citizen to press on the moving bubble will win.

BITCOIN appears in between POTUS ICE CREAM AND THE INTERNET

                BITCOIN
One Bitcoin!

              THE INTERNET
Now ain't that amazing folks!

              THE INTERNET
The Finger app! Just another tool on your financial road to success and don't forgot to sign up for TAPS App. The only app you ever need in remote work!

INT. PHIL'S APARTMENT

Phil is tapping his cellphone and you can tell he has no idea what he is doing.

PHIL'S CELLPHONE

TAPS APP

Phil is tapping on a BLUE BOX that moves an inch every time Phil taps the BLUE BOX.

EXT. FEDERAL COBALT MINING FACILITY

A BLUE TRUCK filled with COBALT drives right off the mountain Cliff with no one in the driver seat.

PHIL'S CELLPHONE

TAPS APP

Phil taps THE BLUE BOX

THE BLUE BOX disappears.

BACK TO THE FINGER APP

>THE INTERNET
And just like that!

>PoTUS ICE CREAM
A tap!

>THE INTERNET
And you just worked all with just a

>POTUS ICE CREAM
Tap!

>THE INTERNET
Tap!

BITCOIN

Bitcoin!

INT. CINDY'S APARTMENT

Cindy's finger finally connects with the

EXT. FEDERAL COBALT MINING FACILITY - CONTINUOUS

THE CHEERING SUBSIDES till you can hear the wind blowing.

THE FINGER from the sky flattens another MINOR.

               MOSES
            (towards Fred)
     Maybe next time kid.

GOD pulls out a ONE-DOLLAR BILL and hands it to ALLAH.

               FRED
   Has anyone ever succeed?

              MOSES
Only two.

81

Floor 8

COBALT

EXT. FEDERAL COBALT MINING FACILITY

FEDERAL ROBOT shines a hologram of the only two successful people in the world that has successfully escape the Cobalt Mining Facility.

A PHOTO OF A WHITE MAN AND BLACK MAN appear side by side.

>   FEDERAL ROBOT
> Freddy Roach and...

>   FRED
> Little hands!

>   FEDERAL ROBOT
> What?

>   FRED
> No no... no... T-REX!

>   FEDERAL ROBOT
> That's not his...

>   FRED
> He looks like a T-REX with his little hands!

Fred starts to laugh so hard that he looks like he's dying.

>   FEDERAL ROBOT
> T-REX?

FRED
T-REX... Get it? Little hand black man. Hey look. I can't reach it.

INT. UNIVERSE - UNKNOWN

ALLAH
That's fucked up!

L. RON HUBBARD
I see it now!

GOD
It's really all in a name.

EXT. FEDERAL COBALT MINING FACILITY - CONTINUOUS

Moses, Fred, and Federal Robot arrive.

THE DEVIL, GOD, ALLAH, BUDDHA, and L. RON HUBBARD are all mining Cobalt while observing Freddy Roach, who is also mining Cobalt in his COCKROACH outfit.

VIVEK, a young Indian, and RODNEY, an old white man, are mining Colbert and overlooking the nearby GODS.

VIVEK
I heard that he can't be killed and he doesn't bleed. He's a GOD!

RODNEY
He's a God dam lab experiment gone wrong. He can be killed. You see this?

Rodney picks up a piece of Cobalt.

RODNEY
This is what runs THE INTERNET.

MOSES
(Towards Fred)
And that.

Moses points at the Colbart that Rodney has in his hands.

MOSES
Is what you need to mine, now get to work. You ain't getting paid to do nothing. So start mining your business.

Moses walks across the sea of MINERS as 6000 MINERS part, making room for Moses to walk through.

THE DEVIL
(pointing at Freddy)
That's our guy!

L. RON HUBBARD
(Typing on his cellphone)
Wait! Are we making a movie or betting on sport?

GOD
What's so special about him?

L. RON HUBBARD
Seriously I forgot.

ALLAH
He can act.

L. RON HUBBARD
Shut up Mohammad, you suck as an actor!

FRED
Is this stuff safe?

VIVEK
Are you dead?

Fred looks around and stares, confused, at Vivek.

FRED
No.

VIVEK
Then common sense would tell you that it's safe.
    (under his breath)
Dumb ass.

BUDDHA
I thought we were playing acting.

ALLAH
    (Towards L. RON HUBBARD)
We're all paid actors, brother.

RODNEY
Very safe...I've been mining for 2,191 days. I never gotten cancer, no flu, and in 6 days, I will finally be free and allowed back into society.

Federal Robot continues to kick ODIN, who is still lying on the floor and enjoying himself.

>   ODIN
> It tickles.

ODIN raises his hand, and a TITANIUM BAT flies into his hands.

>   ODIN
> Batter up!

ODIN stands up and starts to smash the Federal Robot into pieces.

BUDDHA raises his hand.

>   BUDDHA
> Odin, I think it had enough.

>   GOD
> It's not a living being.

>   THE DEVIL
> Just a hunk, a hunk of bent metal.

>   BUDDHA
> All things have feelings.

ODIN stops smashing the Federal Robot.

>   ODIN
> I don't care! This feels good!

>   VIVEK
> That's good to know. I been sentenced to ten years, and I was worried about getting the flu.

Rodney sneezes but not from his face.

> RODNEY
> (hands over Cobalt)
> Hold this. I need to blow my nose.

Rodney opens his shirt button to reveal a BIG NOSE in his chest.

Rodney blows his CHEST NOSE.

> MOSES (O.S.)
> We got a runner!

Floor 9

Highway to hell

Freddy Roach places a big piece of Cobalt in his metal backpack and jumps onto his Ducati motorcycle.

ODIN continues to smash The Federal Robot with his Titanium Bat in one hand while drinking a pint of beer in the other as Freddy drives off.

>			THE DEVIL
>			(Towards L. RON HUBBARD)
> No... this is going to be a combo.

>			L. RON HUBBARD
> I love it, I tell you. I love it!

EXT. FREEWAY 66 - NIGHT - MOVING

"Hellmouth by Bestia Arcana" plays

>			FREDDY ROACH
> I might look funny to you wearing this costume but, it's this cockroach costume that is protecting me from the radiation that emits from the Cobalt. They all have it wrong. They don't listen. I have the tools. I finally have the know how.

SERIES OF FLASHBACKS

A) Freddy is building his custom cellphones.

B) Freddy laser cutting Cobalt

C) Freddy places a piece of Cobalt into his cellphones.

D) Freddy powers on his cell phone.

Freddy Roach, dressed in his COCKROACH outfit, going 106MPH in his Custom built Orange Ducati, zooms passed a

SIGN READS, "WELCOME TO NEWER OAK CITY - CENTER OF FLAT EARTH"

Freddy is holding a custom made working cellphone with one major change.

Freddy pushes a button on the side and out pops a MEDIUM SIZED KNIFE.

> FREDDY ROACH
> They say never bring a knife to a gun fight but, this knife will stop him. I just need to find the right frequency.

Freddy Roach is playing around with the frequency levels on his cellphone.

> FREDDY ROACH
> I'm so close!

EXT. NEWER OAK CITY - NIGHT

SUPER: SEPTEMBER 10, 1974: 9:00 PM NEWER OAK CITY, NEWER OAK

Dark, desolate cloudy city with little lighting.

LOUD SIRENS CAN BE HEARD THROUGHOUT THE CITY

> GOVERNMENT SPEAKERS
> Curfew is in full effect, Go home, or you will be detained for failure to comply.

Multiple Government Drones Follow Freddy who stops in front of THE TWIN TOWERS.

Freddy looking up at the Penthouse.

                FREDDY ROACH
   I will find you.

Freddy pushes a button on the side of the custom made phone and out pops a MEDIUM SIZED KNIFE.

                                    CUT TO:

Floor 10

GNN: GOVERNMENT NEWS NETWORK

TELEVISION

INT. GOVERNMENT NEWS NETWORK STUDIO - NIGHT

> TELEVISION ANNOUNCERS (O.S.)
> It's 9 o'clock, we know where you are, do you? But, first, a message from one of our forced-paid sponsors.

INT. FREDDY ROACH'S APARTMENT - NIGHT

Freddy places a piece of Colbert on all 6 CELLPHONES and each with different frequencies.

> FREDDY ROACH
> One of these gotta work.

Freddy turned on all 6 cellphones, each labeled with its corresponding "WEEKDAY NAME" - SUNDAY'S CELLPHONE is missing.

> CELLPHONE SATURDAY #6 (O.S.)
> Too soon? Twenty-years? It's never too soon.

Freddy Roach is saving a video file while packing his backpack.

His CUSTOM COBALT KNIFE falls out.

> FREDDY ROACH
> That's not good.

                    CELLPHONE #7 (O.S.)
                (continuous)
And losing your hair? Hair plugs for men can get your hair back with confidence. Try Oillyman. And now back to our regular Government sanction News Network channel. GNN News you have to trust.

One of the phones explode.

                    FREDDY ROACH
        I need help.

INT. GOVERNMENT NEWS NETWORK STUDIO - NIGHT

                    HUE.usa.GOV-REPORTER
        And welcome back!

A Chinese Army intelligence wearing a black wig, pretending to be a woman with very noticeable forced slanted eyes.

                    HUE.CHINA.GOV-REPORTER
        It's not like they have a choice. No they don't and onto Bitcoin where it's been steadily climbing and breaking all time records.

                    HUE.usa.GOV-REPORTER
        A lot of people going to be happy.

                    HUE.CHINA.GOV-REPORTER
        Spoke too soon, looks like Bitcoin is staying at that level. A level like no other in this country.

                    HUE.USA.GOV-REPORTER
        Which reminds me. Today we celebrate the 109th anniversary of

                HUE.CHINA.GOV-REPORTER

Just 109?

                HUE.USA.GOV-REPORTER

That's right China co worker of mine. Only 109!

                HUE.CHINA.GOV-REPORTER

Doesn't look a day over 100.

Photo of POTUS ICE CREAM pops on the screen with noticeable hands holding the 91-year-old decrepit President up from behind.

                HUE.USA.GOV-REPORTER

Our savor and beloved President, King POTUS Ice Cream of America, and this portion of the news is brought to you by Flavor One Baskin Robin, The Vanilla Chocolate Chip POTUS edition, and the only flavor.

                HUE.CHINA.GOV-REPORTER

Hope you aren't lactose intolerant.

                HUE.USA.GOV-REPORTER

Hope you still have BITCOIN money.

BOTH HUE.USA And HUE.CHINA belly fake laugh together.

                HUE.USA.GOV-REPORTER
                (Eating Ice Cream)
Thunder will be striking soon!

                HUE.CHINA.GOV-REPORTER

Still amazes me that he is still breathing.

                HUE.USA.GOV-REPORTER

This just in... Bitcoin is on the rise again.

BITCOIN NOTIFICATION RINGS on both of HUE.USA.GOV-REPORTER and HUE.CHINA.GOV-REPORTER.

Both high-five one another.

> NOTIFICATION
> Bitcoin is up 6% in the last hour.

> HUE.USA.GOV-REPORTER
> We can finally afford hot fudge on our presidential chocolate chip cookie ice cream.

> HUE.CHINA.GOV-REPORTER
> It's a blessing.

SILENCE

HUE.USA.GOV-REPORTER and HUE.CHINA.GOV-REPORTER look at one another for a long one second and.

Both Belly fake laugh.

EXT. WASHINGTON AIRPORT - MORNING

THE SECRET SERVICE helps ICE CREAM POTUS, 127-year-old, sit on AIR-FORCE ALWAYS' electric stair lifts.

> HUE.CHINA.GOV-REPORTER (V.O.)
> And look at our president go.

Sitting on the stair lifts, Ice Cream POTUS zips up toward Air-Force Only.

INT. GOVERNMENT NEWS NETWORK STUDIO - CONTINUOUS

HUE.USA.GOV-REPORTER
(Whispering to himself)
That was painful to watch.

HUE.CHINA.GOV-REPORTER
Anyways! On more important news. The Power 3A's. China, Mexico, and America met this morning to discuss the ever-growing population control, economic views facing our planet strip, the ever increasing internet speed that the world is facing and the best tasting POTUS Ice cream now coming in large after public outcry.

HUE.USA.GOV-REPORTER
Isn't it amazing, folk!

HUE.CHINA.GOV-REPORTER
It sure is. No food, our energy infrastructure is crashing, water is running out but chocolate chip Ice Cream in large. What a blessing! Bitcoin now seems like it's taking a dive.

HUE.USA.GOV-REPORTER
And it hasn't rained for decades!

HUE.CHINA.GOV-REPORTER
But who cares! Our internet speed has gotten faster, robust, and more reliable! Here's the man of the dial-up, the spam in your mail, the Capshaw in your heart. THE INTERNET!

The Television splits screen with the reporters on one side and THE INTERNET on the other.

THE INTERNET
Thank you... thank you... thank you...It's great to be hear.

                HUE.CHINA.GOV-REPORTER
It's great to have you on once again and again. Again and again.

                THE INTERNET
Thank you to my supporters.

                HUE.uSA.GOV-REPORTER
So what do you say to the people now talking about this Video Podcaster The Cockroach?

                CUT TO:

SERIES OF SHOTS

A) Citizens of PLANET STRIP all watch COCKROACH online.

B) Freddy Roach, dressed as a, COCKROACH is filming himself next to THE TWIN TOWERS.

C) THE INTERNET see's the video online and roll his eyes with anger.

                BACK TO:

INT. GOVERNMENT NEWS NETWORK STUDIO - CONTINUOUS

THE INTERNET side eyes HUE.USE.GOV-REPORTER

                THE INTERNET
            (laughing)
The Cockroach is just a crazy fan with an outlandish theory, and fact-less claims that are neither true nor based on government scientific research. He's just a trending hashtag that will be squished and forgotten

like his ancestors before him when I wiped them off my heel as I stepped on them as I will do to him.

HUE.USA.GOV-REPORTER
Yeah, um ok... so misinformation?

THE INTERNET
Misinformation? THE INTERNET does not lie!

FREDDY ROACH (O.S.)
Lies!

HUE.CHINA.GOV-REPORTER
And it's true that you are not controlled or in any affiliation with the Power 3A's?

THE INTERNET
I have said this a trillion times, and it's all over my socials. I'm the people's Internet. Yes, I run, control and hold the wealth in the world strip but, without the people. There wouldn't be any need to retain. I wouldn't exist if not for the people and, of course, to our wonderful Government.

HUE.USA.GOV-REPORTER
So this is not true?

SERIES OF SHOTS

A) Freddy Roach puts on his COCKROACH COSTUME

B) Throws one phone on each corner of the NORTH TOWER

C) Turns on cellphone and starts broadcasting

VIDEO OF THE COCKROACH HOUR

Freddy Roach, dressed in a custom-made COCKROACH COSTUME, broadcast his video.

> THE COCKROACH
> No matter how much we make, we will always be in debt to the Government, The Power 3A, who are controlled by The Internet. The only way we can truly be free from slavery. We must kill The Internet!

INT. YOUNG FAMILY'S HOME - CONTINUOUS

A YOUNG COUPLE, sitting on the sofa, glued to their phones.

YOUNG WOMAN, watching THE COCKROACH HOUR on her cell phone, scrolls passed Freddy Roach's posted video.

ON CELLPHONE

> THE COCKROACH
> I need your help to free us from Government control and as many have asked. Yes all your Bitcoin wallets and games would crash if we kill THE INTERNET to be debt free. I know it's hard but, it's the only way to be debt free from government control. Join me.

> YOUNG WOMAN
> Ah hell nawh!

Young Woman scrolls to next video.

CUT TO:

INT. GOVERNMENT NEWS NETWORK STUDIO - CONTINUOUS

     HUE.CHINA.GOV-REPORTER
That makes no sense. No sense!
Why kill THE INTERNET?

     HUE.uSA.GOV-REPORTER
How do you respond to such craziness?

HUE.USA.GOV-REPORTER and HUE.CHINA.GOV-REPORTER WINK at each other.

     THE INTERNET
    (Shaking his head)
No more games, music, movies, or porn? There's no other place in this universe where you can spend all your waking hours wasting away by watching numbness videos until the break of dawn...How awesome is that. But, really, this insect is a moron, the moron of morons!

HUE.USA.GOV-REPORTER pulls out his cell phone and plays games.

     HUE.CHINA.GOV-REPORTER
Hey! Don't forget the Memes. The Memes!

THE INTERNET grabs a USB WIRE and connects to his WEB SERVER from his hand.

     HUE.USA.GOV-REPORTER
And because of you, the world has never been so connected as one. We never have to worry about misinformation because you are the people's Internet.

HUE.CHINA.GOV-REPORTER is texting a MEME.

                  HUE.CHINA.GOV-REPORTER
What do you have to say to the people that call you addicting and self-absorbing?

HUE.USA.GOV-REPORTER'S STOMACH IS THUNDERING

                  THE INTERNET
                  (Eating Ice Cream)
Addicting and self-absorbing?... Sounds like the people love me!

THE SCREEN SPLITS INTO THREE

BITCOIN POPS ON SCREEN.

                  BITCOIN
It's me a Bitcoin and I'm moving on up.

BITCOIN throws glitter up in the air and the SCREEN shrinks back to TWO.

                  THE INTERNET
Bitcoin is such a character.

BITCOIN runs back to the screen and throws glitter up in the air.

                  BITCOIN
I'm moving on up!

BITCOIN disappears from the screen.

BITCOIN NOTIFICATION SOUND DING DING DING

NOTIFICATION
Congrats! You just earned one Bitcoin!

THE INTERNET
I love that guy!

FLOOR 11

THE POWER 3

INT. PENTAGON - MORNING

The POWER 3A BOARDROOM are covered in RFID Signal WI-FI Shield

                  POTUS ICE CREAM
I fucking hate him!

                  MEXICA PRESIDENT
Lower your voice. He can hear us.

                  SUPREME CHINA LEADER
Not when we are in this RFID Signal WI-FI shielding room. Our conversations can finally be private and not like last time.

THE POWER 3A views an empty chair.

                  POTUS ICE CREAM
Remember Mexica?

                  MEXICA PRESIDENT
It's Mexico! Mexico! Mexicooooooo!

                  SUPREME CHINA LEADER
Relax Hombre.

                  MEXICA PRESIDENT
Relax? Is your country called EL Chino? No!... He wiped every piece of information on the Internet, and now people don't even remember Mexico use to be spelled M.E.X.I.C.O! Mexico... Not! Mexic...A!

> POTUS ICE CREAM
> Calm down, Fidel. Remember what happened to Russia.

THE POWER 3A looks at an empty chair again.

> MEXICA PRESIDENT
> (Spanish)
> Remember? We need to kill that son of a bitch! Today!

> POTUS ICE CREAM
> And who's stupid enough to try?

> SUPREME CHINA LEADER
> Everyone seems to forget that he's radioactive. Anyone that comes near him has a 96% chance of dying. Only four people of thousands that have gotten close survived!

> MEXICA PRESIDENT
> Does he know he es radioactive?

> SUPREME CHINA LEADER
> Of course he knows. Don't you read your briefs?

Four SCREENS APPEAR with each screen displaying a bio of: THE INTERNET, SIRI, ALEXA, DJ JILL.MP3.

POTUS ICE CREAM pulls out his cell phone and starts dialing.

> SUPREME CHINA LEADER
> And who might you be calling?

> POTUS ICE CREAM
> The Devil.

SUPREME CHINA LEADER
How the hell do you have his phone number?

POTUS ICE CREAM
We went to elementary school together back in the day.

THE DEVIL appears in the form of HUE.

THE DEVIL
(Towards POTUS ICE CREAM)
What the fuck do you want?

POTUS ICE CREAM
What? We aren't friends no longer?

THE DEVIL
What the fuck do you want?

POTUS ICE CREAM
Devil buddy o' pal.

THE DEVIL grabs POTUS ICE CREAM by the collar.

THE DEVIL
Get to the fucking point, you fuck. Fuck!

POTUS ICE CREAM
Kill THE INTERNET!

THE DEVIL
Sorry. I no longer do that kind of work.

POTUS ICE CREAM
What do you mean? You're THE DEVIL!

> THE DEVIL
> Just because I'm THE DEVIL doesn't make me THE DEVIL.

> GOD (O.S.)
> Talk about confusing the fuck out of you.

> ALLAH (O.S.)
> And they say I have issues.

> THE DEVIL
> I outsource all of my killings now. Just too much fucking work. What's in it for me besides owning all your souls already?

> POTUS ICE CREAM
> Free Chocolate Chip Ice Cream for life!

> THE DEVIL
> I'm lactose intolerant, asshole!

> MEXICA PRESIDENT
> My wife.

THE DEVIL throws up.

> SUPREME CHINA LEADER
> My Netflix password account.

> THE DEVIL
> What about Amazon and Disney+

> SUPREME CHINA LEADER
> I'll throw in my Masterclass subscription for good measure.

> THE DEVIL
> You drive a hard bargain missy.

            POTUS ICE CREAM
Well do we have a deal?

            THE DEVIL
What is needed?

            POTUS ICE CREAM
We need THE INTERNET dead and pronto, chief.

            THE DEVIL
I told you dumb-fuck. I outsource my work now.
Losing your hearing?

            MEXICA PRESIDENT
Get someone that Can't fail.

THE DEVIL stops and gives MEXICA PRESIDENT the finger point of yes. You are onto something there.

THE DEVIL gives out a big smile.

            THE DEVIL
I know, just the man! He's Cant fail because he always GetRite!

            POTUS ICE CREAM
Sounds like the man I want! What's his name?

FLOOR 12

CANTGETRITE

          THE DEVIL
CantGetRite!

          Cantgetrite (O.S.)
So apparently, I'm the man who's stupid enough to try with only a 6% chance of making it out alive.
          (beat)
Well, fuck me.

EXT. NEWER OAK - NIGHT

A SHOOTING STAR appears in the skies.

          FREDDY ROACH (O.S.)
I wish…

INT. CANTGETRITE'S HOME - DAY

          CANTGETRITE (O.S.)
No, I didn't wake up on the wrong side. I just should have paid more attention.

Out of the smoke and fire emerges, CANTGETRITE, dressed in a GQ suit holding onto a Credit Report Letter and dancing to "Janet Jackson's The Pleasure Principles" while grabbing his NEW BMW KEYS.

CantGetRite pulls out his Vape and takes one big hit.

CantGetRite quickly looks around and immediately grabs his Credit Report Letter with both hands.

CU - CREDIT REPORT LETTER

850 CantGetRite's Credit Score

> CANTGETRITE
> (kissing the letter)
> Yes!

CantGetRite dances his way toward the Door.

INT. CANTGETRITE'S BMW - MOVING - MORNING

> CANTGETRITE (V.O.)
> Yeah… that's me. Hey, don't hate. Congratulate. I was happy! Only in America, where you can wake up debt free and be back in worser debt then before and just in time for lunch. My stupid ass decided to get a degree in social political science. Six days after graduating, in hindsight, I thought I was a genius then I got arrested for possession and intent to sell crystal meth. Yeah muthafucka, you heared that shit right. Don't be pretending you're deaf now. I already have a blind friend. Not looking to add to my handicap.

CantGetRite takes out his vape and smokes while making a left turn on 6th and WAY STREET.

CantGetRite passes The Federal Court House building and sticks out his middle finger.

> CANTGETRITE (V.O.)
> I smoke cannabis because of the stress of it all, and it's cheaper than killing someone. Even thou I spent more time in jail than a child killer. That's ok. We got the black man that will take the fall for selling Crystal when in fact it's good o' daddy, The Chief of police to

protect his sorry ass son but, I'm trying to let go. I didn't even know what Crystal meth looked like till they showed it in my possessions. Cops these days are also magicians of sorts. Hey look here it's a gun. Now how did that get there. Abracadabra you get fine. Hocus Pocus and half your check just disappears to some uncle you never met that claims to do this all for the greater good of man kind while giving you the creeps.

CANTGETRITE looks directly at the CAMERA.

> CANTGETRITE
> (While vaping)

I bet you your own two cents that you would smoke if you went through what I went through. I don't mean to rant but, the weed hasn't kicked in yet and I'm just pissed because even in my sleep. My sleep of all things. I feel like I'm working none stop. I dream work. No not the what you think. Literally dream work. One time I swear that I was a doctor delivering a baby and it had to be a dream. Didn't know a baby can be such a fuckin' bitch!

INT. FEDERAL COURT HOUSE - DAY

CANTGETRITE - DAYDREAMING

CantGetRite stands up and looks the Judge dead in the eye.

> CANTGETRITE (V.O.)

Sometimes, I have no clue what I'm thinking or saying. Just too busy making bread. I really want to bitch slap this judge.

GOD, THE DEVIL, ALLAH, BUDDHA, ODIN and L. RON HUBBARD appear on the Judge's shoulders, looking like flies.

A CAT runs across the room.

> CANTGETRITE (V.O.)
> Was that a fucking cat?

> JUDGE
> I see we have another degenerate before me.

> CANTGETRITE
> You judgmental prick! You think you can sit on your high chair and tell everyone that they're wrong, like you, are so righteous. Which God gave you the right bitch ass motherfucker!

CantGetRite is just tapping his feet back and forth in stress.

> CANTGETRITE (V.O.)
> I took an edible for this reason and it's not kicking in. I think I smoke too much that... oh wait.

CantGetRite takes a very big deep breath.

> CANTGETRITE (V.O.)
> It's about time.

CantGetRite is enjoying his high with a smile knowing that it's going to be his last for an unknown amount of time but, he's ok with it.

CU - JUDGE'S LEFT SHOULDER

GOD slowly raises his hand while holding THE BIBLE upside down in the other hand.

The other GODS applaud as GOD does his "HAPPY DANCE."

> CANTGETRITE
> Fuck you...Fuck you...Fuck you... Fuck you...Fuck you...Fuck you.

All the GODS were aghast.

INT. FEDERAL COURT HOUSE - CONTINUOUS

> CANTGETRITE (V.O.)
> (Clears his throat)
> What I really told the Judge...

> CANTGETRITE
> Your honor, with much due respect. Those drugs. Those drugs are not mine, and I do not have any knowledge of to whom they belong too. If it were weed, then I would agree that it could possibly be mine, and heck, if it was cocaine, then there might be somewhat of a hint of possibility it might be mine but meth? That there is a defiantly, no way Jose in hell's chance ever. That's a white man's drug!
> (beat)
> Your Honor.

CU - JUDGE'S RIGHT SHOULDER

THE DEVIL, ODIN, BUDDHA, ALLAH, and L.RON HUBBARD are fanning GOD, who is overly play-acting "dying"

> JUDGE
> After hearing all the evidence and the defendant as well as his racist remarks.

                    CANTGETRITE
Racist?

CantGetRite starts to hallucinate and finds himself tied to a BURNING CROSS and the JUDGE now wearing a KKK Outfit.

                    JUDGE
The court decides to withdraw the intent to sell, but CantGetRite, you are hear by found guilty of possession. I do believe that you had no intention to sell but, a racist remark is racist at heart and, a drug user is always a drug user.

CantGetRite is on fire but, is so pissed off that he isn't showing any pain.

                    CANTGETRITE
Weed is not a drug!

JUDGE slams his gavel.

                    JUDGE
Quiet in the courtroom!

                    CANTGETRITE
And I didn't say anything racist!

Judge slams his gavel.

                    JUDGE
Oh is that a fact boy!

CantGetRite nods his head.

                    CANTGETRITE
I would say go fuck yourself but, I don't think you can even see your pee with all that lard in front of you.

JUDGE
Court Reporter. Tell me what the illiterate cotton picker murder the clean air around me with his stench of though that poison the air we breathe.

COURT REPORTER stops typing.

COURT REPORTER
Yes, your honor.

JUDGE
Would you please read back what he said to the courts.

Court Reporter looks through the sheets.

COURT REPORTER
I ain't no racist, you fucking piece of white trailer trash. Fuck yo mama, fuck yo daddy and fuck yo bald head granny. Die… die you miserable old motherfucker. Die! I'm going to fuck you up bitch!

JUDGE
You are sentenced to a maximum of 6 years in federal prison.

CANTGETRITE
6 years!?

JUDGE
I need order in the court!

CANTGETRITE
I'm going give you an order. You best wait for me bitch!

JUDGE
Order!

Judge hitting the gavel as hard as he can on the table.

                    CANTGETRITE
          Really? 6 years?

You can see CantGetRite's eyes just slowly lower in frustration.

FLASH OF LIGHT

CantGetRite is no longer on a burning cross and the Judge is back his normal self.

FLASH OF LIGHT

CantGetRite's face is stunned and in complete silence.

FLASH OF LIGHT

                    CANTGETRITE
          What the fuck is going on?

                    GOD (O.S.)
          Are you sure this is the guy?

                    THE DEVIL (O.S.)
          Are you sure?

A CAT walks across the screen.

                    KAREN (O.S.)
          I told you that's the guy!

FLOOR 13

WORKIN' PRETENDER

EXT. FEDERAL COURT HOUSE - DAY

        CANTGETRITE (V.O.)
And six years later. Having a useless degree in social political science, and over one hundred thousand dollars in student tuition debt. Lose all my possessions, can't get a job being a federal felon, yet they still tax my ass... Now ain't that but a catch 22-bitch!
    (beat)
Oh I feel another rant coming along and yeah I work like a slave but, working in your sleep while asleep and having a job that pays you while you are sleeping is just a mindfuck no less but, why the fuck. What the fuck. Its like money just disappears. The only people to ever write me while locked up was my good o' friend Grant but, I always had a hard time reading his handwriting and I know he meant well but, it always looks like if a dog wrote it. And my mom.

SERIES OF SHOTS of CantGetRite working numerous jobs.

        CANTGETRITE (V.O.)
Luckily for me. My mom Jemima took care of me at age six, and if it wasn't for her. I be jobless, homeless, God knows what else-less. Even now, she's taking care of me. She owns Jemima's Temps. My mom is incredible. She can get anyone a job.

INT. JEMIMA'S TEMPS - DAY

CantGetRite takes a picture of JEMIMA RITE, 66 black women, with 59 of her Jamaican clients and 1 Mexican.

> CANTGETRITE (V.O.)
> Here I am taking a photo of her with 60 of her clients, all Jamaicans except for Jose.

JOSE, THE MEXICAN, smiles at the camera.

> CANTGETRITE (V.O.)
> And all of us are gainfully employed and happy because of Jemima Rite.

OFFICE BUILDING

> OFFICE MANAGER
> (Off of Cant's documents)
> You're Thomas McBrain?

> CANTGETRITE
> Yes.

HOSPITAL SURGERY ROOM

> DOCTOR KNIGHT
> (Off of Cant's documents)
> Are you Doctor Wee?

> CANTGETRITE
> (Vietnamese)
> Yes.

> CANTGETRITE (V.O)
> You might be thinking how the hell can a black man fake it so good? I been telling you son, that I been dream working and you just don't believe me. Image

if you would. You studying to be a dancer yet you have no feet but, when you are sleeping. You're the main dancer on the nut cracker and this would be my 6th heart transplant. I even was the president but, I always wake up right before the alien invasion.

NURSE #1
It's time Doctors!

DOCTOR KNIGHT
Ok. Heart transplant in six minutes. Prep time.

CANTGETRITE
(Spanish)
Yes Doctor.

CANTGETRITE (V.O.)
If there's a job, I'm the man that can do it!... And for the record. I didn't say that to the judge, and I just said it in my head.

SILENCE

CANTGETRITE
Oh and one last thing I forgot. Fuck that cracker of a judge.

INT. CANTGETRITE'S BEDROOM

CantGetRite wakes up.

CANTGETRITE
Now what!

CantGetRite jumps out of bed and into

INT. HOSPITAL DELIVERY ROOM - MORNING

Everything in the room screams a different era.

                      NURSE #1
               (looking at CantGetRite)
    You're a doctor?

CantGetRite looks at himself and notices he is dressed up in hospital gear with a name tag that reads, "Doctor Can't"

                    CANTGETRITE
    I guess, I am.

                      NURSE #1
    But, you're black!

SERIES OF SHOTS

A) Mother in the Delivery Room is screaming

B) The BABY is shot in the air

C) CantGetRite catches the Baby in the air by her left foot

D) A Cat walks between CantGetRite's legs

                    KAREN (O.S.)
    That's him! I finally found him!

                  THE DEVIL (O.S.)
    Good we have confirmation finally.

CantGetRite is holding the baby upside down by the left leg.

                    CANTGETRITE
    Do you have a name?

                    MOTHER (O.S.)
Yes.

                    CANTGETRITE
          What's the baby's name?

CantGetRite slaps the baby in the ass.

                    KAREN (V.O.)
No!

                                        CUT TO:

FLOOR 14

MEDICAL BILL

INT. HOSPITAL WAITING ROOM - DAY

CantGetRite sits down with his hands holding up his head while holding the hospital bill.

A massive painting of RAMON RAMON, Head of the Hospital, hangs on the wall behind CantGetRite.

          HOSPITAL BILLING (V.O.)
  We do offer payment arrangements.

INT. HOSPITAL - DAY

ICU ROOM 6

JEMIMA RITE, 66 black woman lying on the hospital bed with multiple tubes plugged into her frail body.

              JEMIMA RITE
  Keep your head up, son. I will be alright.

              Cantgetrite
  How can you be so positive.

              JEMIMA RITE
It always work out in the end ; if it doesn't, it's not the end.

HALLWAY

                    DOCTOR WAYNE
                  (Towards CantGetRite)
I'm sorry, but Mrs. Rite won't make it to the end of the day without this procedure.

BILLING DEPARTMENT

                    HOSPITAL BILLING
The Hospital can't perform the surgery without full payment.

ICU ROOM 6

                      JEMIMA RITE
    Jesus will save me.

Out of now where A CAT jumps on Jemima Rite's lap

GOD dressed up as SUPERMAN flies towards Jemina and lands on her afro.

CantGetRite, unable to hide his distaste, pulls out his Weed Vape and takes a hit, not caring what anyone will say.

Jemima Rite extends her hands towards CantGetRite.

GOD, dressed up as MC HAMMER, starts dancing all around Jemina's afro.

                      JEMIMA RITE
    Let's pray.

Jemima and the CAT are like best friends. The CAT is sleeping on her lap.

CU - CANTGETRITE'S FACE

CantGetRite is annoyed.

> CANTGETRITE
> Yes, let's pray that he calls us with his credit card details.

CantGetRite holds Jemima's frail hand.

> CANTGETRITE (O.S.)
> Fuck GOD.

CUT TO:

INT. UNIVERSE - UNKNOWN

GOD starts walking towards CantGetRite's world portal dressed up as THE PUNISHER.

> GOD
> Oh, those are some fighting words!

Odin efficiently stops GOD from walking any further with his HAMMER.

CUT TO:

FLOOR 15

MANIPULATION

INT. HOSPITAL WAITING ROOM

CU - CANGETRITE'S FACE

> THE DEVIL (O.S.)
> I couldn't help but hear that you are require some financial assistance.

The CAT jumps onto THE DEVIL'S lap.

BACK TO:

INT. HOSPITAL WAITING ROOM

CantGetRite looks up to see HUE, 67, Charming, charismatic, well style, alluring polished 5'9" handsome Asian gentleman who is blind and holding a WHITE CANE.

THE DEVIL is disguised as HUE.

HUE/DEVIL sense CantGetRite's silence.

> HUE/DEVIL
> I'm blind, not deaf son.

ICU ROOM 6

> JEMIMA RITE
> You got to learn to walk by faith, not by sight.

> CANTGETRITE
> GOD is not going to save you!

      JEMIMA RITE
You still don't understand. We are all GODS in his eyes.

      CANTGETRITE
     (mumbles to himself)
Thank God, I'm an atheist.

WAITING ROOM

CantGetRite's Cellphone DINGS!

CU - CANTGETRITE'S CELLPHONE

TEXT MESSAGE from GRANT DAVIS: "Sorry to hear about your mom, I'm here if you need me emoji heart, bow and arrow."

          BACK TO SCENE

      THE DEVIL
Got to love The Internet and all of its technological advancement. Can you imagine life without the Internet?

      CANTGETRITE
     (not paying attention)
Yeah.

CantGetRite taps the thumbs up on Grant Davis' message.

      CANTGETRITE (V.O.)
Here I am... talking to a blind man and I just thumbs up a message from another blind man. Like what in the fuckin' Eyes' is going on here?

CantGetRite pulls out his vape and takes a hit.

                CANTGETRITE (V.O.)
He's not going to know.

                THE DEVIL
I'm sorry to interrupt you...I get so passionate when I can't see the possibilities know that you're someone special. We can help each other.

                CANTGETRITE
We?

CantGetRite gets startled as he sees THE DEVIL for the first time.

                CANTGETRITE
What the fuck are you?

                THE DEVIL
I know what would help ease your concerns. Out of good faith and I believe you can deliver. I'll take care of Mrs.

THE DEVIL tilts his head towards the Hospital Billing Department window.

                THE DEVIL
What's her name, Maria?

                HOSPITAL BILLING/MARIA (O.S.)
                (Yelling at THE DEVIL)
Jemima Rite!

                THE DEVIL
                (Toward CantgetRite)
I'll take care of Mrs. Rite's medical bill so that she can have her life-saving operation and you can fully

commit to helping me without the worry and stress of coming up with the funds right away.

THE DEVIL tilts his head towards the Hospital Billing Department window.

> THE DEVIL
> Route it to my personal billing Maria!

> HOSPITAL BILLING/MARIA (O.S.)
> No problem Mr. Ramon!

> CANTGETRITE
> You're Ramon Ramon?

CantGetRite looks behind him and sees a large painting of RAMON RAMON, looking to be in his 30s, with the title, "Ramon Ramon: Head of Hospital."

> CANTGETRITE
> Wait wait wait.

> THE DEVIL
> Yeah...

> CANTGETRITE
> Would you pick a fucking body to stay as because I'm getting confused to who the hell I'm speaking too.

> THE DEVIL
> You're speaking to the king of hells.

DOCTOR KNIGHT and JOSE, THE MEXICAN, dressed as an EMT run passed CantGetRite and THE DEVIL towards

the emergency room, while pushing an injured black man on a gurney.

      DOCTOR KNIGHT
Hey Doctor Wee!

      CANTGETRITE
    (German)
Hey Doctor Knight!

THE DEVIL turns into Jermima

      THE DEVIL
How about this?

      CANTGETRITE
If you're going to fuck with me mentally, I'm going to walk.

      THE DEVIL
I see. Straight to the point.

      CANTGETRITE
Can you please.

THE DEVIL changes back to THE DEVIL form.

      THE DEVIL
Are you happy now little princess.

      CANTGETRITE
No because you want something that I can't afford.

      THE DEVIL
Don't be so judgmental. Maybe I just wanted to pop by the universe of hell you live in just to say. Hi

CantGetRite. How's it hanging? No. I did not waste my god dam time to mess with you. I have a proposition for you. A job. A way for you to pay off all your debt and as a bonus. I'll help your little Jermima live a fruitful life and you have no worries.

                  CANTGETRITE
Sounds too good to be true.

                  THE DEVIL
It's up to you. I ain't going to push you. Just remember that the offer still stands because I do care.

INT. UNIVERSE

                  L. RON HUBBARD
Wait a minute now... wait just a minute. Something just doesn't sound right?

                  THE DEVIL
Of course it doesn't

A CAT walks passed L. RON HUBBARD.

                  BUDDHA
What do you expect for the man of mischief.

                  ALLAH
A good show.

                  ODIN
What's going on.

                  GOD
Yeah I'm starting to sense it but, can't put my finger on it.

GOD SNEEZES

                    GOD
          Is there a cat around?

                                    CUT TO:

FLOOR 16

RAMON RAMON

INT. HOSPITAL ROOM - DAY

Jermima Rite's room.

NURSE gives CantGetRite some medical pamphlets.

                  NURSE #1
            (whispers to CantGetRite)
    Incase you can't.

Nurse #1 turns on the room's television and immediately exits.

                JEMIMA RITE
    Can't what dear?

TELEVISION

THE DEVIL is playing RAMON RAMON on the Hospital's room television.

                  THE DEVIL
            (Towards the camera)
    Paying your hospital bills is a big responsibility that we know can be detrimental on you, your family and us if you don't pay.

                CANTGETRITE (O.S.)
    Oh, come on! A medical video on bills?

                JEMIMA RITE
    Oh, hush!

> (whispering to herself)
> He sure is handsome.

THE DEVIL
At Ramon Ramon Medical, we'll treat you like family and extend our 100% payment plans so that you can worry about living and not worry about dying because a dead family member is a non-paying member.

ICU ROOM 6

ALL THE GODS are dancing to "Oppa Gangnam Style by PSY."

JEMIMA RITE
See. Everything works out. Stop stressing over money. It will kill you if you keep thinking about it.

ODIN
He sure is having fun.

GOD
That's the devil in him.

ALLAH
It's been educational.

BUDDHA just sighs.

L. RON HUBBARD
Well looks like we'll learn more about his grand master plan.

ALLAH
I hope so because I'm not in the mood to wait any longer.

ODIN
I hear ya.

CUT TO:

BILLING DEPARTMENT

HOSPITAL BILLING/MARY
Unfortunately, Jemima Rite doesn't qualify for our hospital family plan.

CANTGETRITE
But the video says...

HOSPITAL BILLING/MARY
(pointing to the sign in front)
We can no longer extend our family payment plans. That video is over two decades old.

CANTGETRITE
What about me?

HOSPITAL BILLING/MARY
Unfortunately, we can not give any credit to known criminals, alive or dead.

CANTGETRITE
I did my time and have a perfect credit score!

HOSPITAL BILLING/MARY
Sorry but it's hospital policy. Here are few third-party loan agencies that can possibly help, and here is today's itemized bill for her current stay.

CANTGETRITE
(looking at the bill)
Oh, come on!

THE DEVIL
Wow that's a big bill.

FLOOR 17

GOOGLE ME

INT. HOSPITAL HALLWAY - DAY

CantGetRite walks slowly towards the hallway chairs and looks up to see a huge captions. "You are more than a patient. You're family".

> CANTGETRITE
> Fuck yo family!

CANTGETRITE'S FLASHBACK

EXT. JEMIMA RITE'S HOUSE - MORNING

Jemima Rite picks up a YOUNG CANTGETRITE.

> JEMIMA RITE
> Never go after fast money. Easy money is never good money.

CU - YOUNG CANTGETRITE'S EYES

END OF CANTGETRITE'S FLASHBACK

CU - CANGETRITE'S EYES

BACK TO SCENE:

INT. HOSPITAL HALLWAY - DAY

CANTGETRITE is sitting on one of the Hallway chairs, looking up at RAMON RAMON.

THE DEVIL appears

> THE DEVIL
> You sound like a strapping young lad who isn't afraid of a challenge. It wouldn't take you long.

> CANTGETRITE
> What do I have to do in simple terms.

> THE DEVIL
> Oh the direct approach. It's been awhile.

THE DEVIL pulls out a six million dollar check.

> THE DEVIL
> I need you to give this to my mortal son Freddy.

> CANTGETRITE
> Never heard of Venmo? Cashapp?

> THE DEVIL
> He's not a smart kid.

> CANTGETRITE
> Ever though of mailing him a money order?

> THE DEVIL
> He just got my looks.

> CANTGETRITE
> That just sounds too easy. What else?

> THE DEVIL
> Wow you sure are the party pooper.

> CANTGETRITE
> I been fucked over and I ain't getting played by you.

THE DEVIL
Like if you had a choice in the manner. Let me remind you that all I ask is for you to be a delivery boy and your debt and your beautiful mom will survive and be alive for many more wonderful years.

CANTGETRITE
What else?

THE DEVIL
Dam you aren't fun when you ain't high as fuck.

CANTGETRITE
What else!

THE DEVIL pulls out a vape and hands it to CantGetRite.

THE DEVIL
I usually ain't this friendly but, you seem like you need this now. You're too up tight and it's messing with my mood.

CANTGETRITE
And what else?

THE DEVIL
Smoke the dam vape.

CantGetRite takes a big drag out of the vape.

There's silence in the room as CantGetRite fully relaxes.

CANTGETRITE
What else besides wasting my time to deliver something that you can easily do with usps

THE DEVIL
And you have to Kill The Internet.

CANTGETRITE
Da fuck?

Silence in the room. You can hear a niddle drop.

CANTGETRITE
So find someone, give him a check and kill his internet? Like unplugging the what the what?

THE DEVIL
Yeah something like that. Keep smoking.

CantGetRite takes another hit from THE DEVIL'S VAPE and has been making CantGetRite a little bit too high.

CANTGETRITE
Kill the internet? Why stop there. Lets kill the music.

THE DEVIL
Good idea

CANTGETRITE
Sure what ever.

THE DEVIL
You have six days to complete and if you don't then you will owe the debt plus your poor old mother won't live to see another day as her sickness will just get worse and worse every day til she dies all because you couldn't afford to pay the medical bill for the life saving surgery that she needs it but, you are worthless and you continue to be worthless if you don't take the deal.

CANTGETRITE
Fine.
    (beat)
Fuck you!

THE DEVIL hands CantGetRite his tablet with a contract.

          THE DEVIL
Let's make this legal, shall we?

CantGetRite looks at the tablet's document.

          CANTGETRITE
Nueva? Looks like there's a misspelling on your document.

          THE DEVIL
No, it's spelled right. I assure you. NEWER OAK is on the South side of New York, the hotter side.

THE DEVIL extends his hand towards CantGetRite

INT. UNIVERSE

          ODIN
Oh I got it!

150

FLOOR 18

DEAL

INT. HOSPITAL ROOM - MORNING

Jemima extends her weak hands at CantGetRite.

CantGetRite holds her hand.

> CANTGETRITE
> You're going to be alright. I secured the funding for your operation.

THE DEVIL, GOD, ALLAH, ODIN, BUDDHA, and L.RON HUBBARD appear on Jemima Rite's shoulder in flea sized.

> JEMIMA RITE
> Hallelujah, praise be Jesus Christ!

The CAT jumps out of Jemima's lap and runs out the door.

CU - JEMIMA RITE'S RIGHT SHOULDER

Everyone gives GOD a high-five.

> GOD
> That's right bitch... HallelfuckingYeah! Praise be me mutherfucking bitches.

GOD is the only one dancing on Jemima Rite's shoulder.

> THE DEVIL
> You do know. I'm the one that made the contract.

> L. RON HUBBARD
> Indeed

GOD (O.S.)
Ah yeah... who's the bitch now!

L. RON HUBBARD
Was that necessary? Are you doin' drugs again?

ALLAH
Edibles from my far in Pakistan.

GOD AND ALLAH HIGH-FIVE ONE ANOTHER

BUDDHA
Kids.

CUT TO:

INT. HOSPITAL HALLWAY - DAY

CU - THE DEVIL'S HAND

CANTGETRITE (V.O.)
Ok, recap Cant... some old Asian dude who owns multiple Hospital in the California area wants you to travel to someplace in New York to find his son who wants nothing to do with him yet convince him to take this 6 million dollar check before it expires in 6 days. If I can track him down during the flight, find him, give him this check. I can be back before...

THE DEVIL
What do you say?

CANTGETRITE
Fuck it.

THE DEVIL hands CantGetRite the Return to Sender Check.

                    THE DEVIL
That's the spirit!

                    CANTGETRITE
You couldn't even wire him through crypto?

                    HUE/DEVIL/RAMON RAMON
He's not the smartest egg of mine.

                    CANTGETRITE (V.O.)
I can defiantly do this in a day.

CantGetRite looks at the 6 million dollar check in amazement.

                    CANTGETRITE (V.O.)
And who can say no to this bad boy!

                    CANTGETRITE
Let me get this straight. All I have to do is give
        (reading the check)
Freddy Roach, this check and get paid sixty-six thousand dollars plus my mom's medical bills taken care of as long as I do this within 6 days?

THE DEVIL is changing to HUE, THE DEVIL, RAMON RAMON, and back to HUE, yet CantGetRite doesn't see this.

                    HUE/DEVIL/RAMON RAMON
Sounds like a great Deal?

The Cat walks between CantGetRite's leg.

                    CANTGETRITE
Deal!

FLOOR 19

HIGH-FIVE

FREEZE FRAME

GOD, ALLAH, ODIN, BUDDHA, and L. RON HUBBARD appear.

　　　　　　　ALLAH
　　This plan makes no sense!

　　　　　　　BUDDHA
　　I'm confused just as much.

　　　　　　　THE DEVIL
　　It's not… suppose.

　　　　　　　GOD
　　Then what is it?

FLOOR 20

L. RON HUBBARD

>   ODIN
> It's
>   (Glances at L.RON HUBBARD)
> Just a way to confuse the audience that is reading this crap in an attempt to solidify that he knows and understands that he's crazy.
>   (towards L.RON HUBBARD)
> Close enough?

L.RON HUBBARD stops typing and looks directly at the CAMERA, breaking the 4TH WALL.

>   L. RON HUBBARD
> Something just doesn't feel kosher.

CU - HANDSHAKE

>   CANTGETRITE (V.O.)
> Dam his hand is hot!

HUE/DEVIL/RAMON RAMON extends his hand down, reaching for a high-five.

ALLAH, GOD, ODIN, BUDDHA, and L.RON HUBBARD, looking like mosquitos, fly down and high-five HUE/DEVIL/RAMON RAMON

L. RON HUBBARD grabs one of his books and flips it backwards making him go back into time.

INT. SOUTH TOWER LOBBY - DAY

USPS POSTAL MAN appears him THE DEVIL'S FACE

USPS POSTAL MAN
Have a package for GODS INC.

THE DEVIL'S POV

          THE DEVIL (O.S.)
Da fuck man, don't you even knock?

THE PACKAGE is from THE INTERNET and the return address reads: "#1 PENTHOUSE, NORTH TOWER

          THE DEVIL
Guys... I Have an idea.

GOD, BUDDHA, ALLAH, ODIN, and L. RON HUBBARD stop in their tracks.

BUDDHA is the only one shaking his head.

L. RON HUBBARD walks up to THE DEVIL and yanks THE PACKAGE from his hands and pulls out a LETTER from THE INTERNET.

L. RON HUBBARD reading the LETTER

          L. RON HUBBARD
Subject Application to join GODS INC. Jeez this guy.

L. RON HUBBARD looks closer at the letter.

THE LETTER

Subject: Application to Join Gods Inc. and the Gods Union

Dear Gods Inc.,

I am writing to formally request membership in Gods Inc. and the Gods Union under the designation "THE INTERNET." I believe that my unique qualities and capabilities make me a

suitable candidate to join the ranks of the divine entities under your esteemed organization.

Here are the reasons why I believe I would make an exceptional addition to Gods Inc.:

Speed: I operate at unprecedented speeds, connecting billions of individuals worldwide instantaneously. My ability to transmit information and data across vast distances in milliseconds is unparalleled.

Downloads: I facilitate the seamless transfer and retrieval of vast amounts of knowledge, entertainment, and resources. My infrastructure supports billions of downloads daily, empowering users globally.

Bitcoin and Digital Economy: I am intricately involved in the digital economy, including the management and transfer of cryptocurrencies like Bitcoin. My network facilitates transactions securely and efficiently, underpinning modern financial systems.

Global Reach and Accessibility: I transcend physical boundaries, providing access to information and services to individuals regardless of geographical location. My network is inclusive and accessible to billions, promoting connectivity and communication worldwide.

Innovation and Adaptability: I continuously evolve and adapt to meet the ever-changing needs of users and technological advancements. My infrastructure supports the integration of cutting-edge technologies, ensuring reliability and efficiency.

I am eager to contribute my capabilities to the Gods Union, promoting connectivity, knowledge sharing, and digital empowerment on a global scale. I am committed to upholding the values of innovation, accessibility, and interconnectedness that define the modern era.

Thank you for considering my application. I look forward to the opportunity to serve as a member of Gods Inc. and contribute to its mission.

Yours sincerely,

THE INTERNET

L. RON HUBBARD'S Face starts to twitch

>BUDDHA
Did you find something wrong with the letter?

>L. RON HUBBARD
No, the letter was written very well.

>THE DEVIL
Then what's the issue doc?

>GOD
How did that douche bag write such a nice letter?

>ALLAH
Than who?

>L. RON HUBBARD
ChatGPT!

>GOD
Are you sure?

>L. RON HUBBARD
Are you gay?

>GOD
No.

              L. RON HUBBARD
We went to the same school and I can recognize that cheater's style of writing anywhere.

              ALLAH
If this is true than THE INTERNET'S application will be disqualify.

              THE DEVIL
You guys don't think THE INTERNET is capable of writing a professional letter?

GOD, ALLAH, BUDDHA, ODIN, AND L. RON HUBBARD SCREAM NO! AT THE SAME TIME.

              THE DEVIL
Well. I'll be so shocked!

              L. RON HUBBARD
Rules are rules.

              BUDDHA
L. RON will investigate it.

              ODIN
I'll go with you.

THE DEVIL pulls out his cellphone and clicks on THE INTERNET'S MESSAGE.

              THE DEVIL
Well it was fun while it lasted.

              GOD
On the brightside, there's a lot more ways to play a game.

     THE DEVIL
   (mouthing to himself)
 You are so right!

THE DEVIL has been messaging THE INTERNET this whole time, warning about L. RON HUBBARD, visiting him.

INT. PENTHOUSE - MORNING

SIRI NOTIFICATION BING

      SIRI
 Hey babe! There's finally an opening to GODS INC.

      ALEXA
 Yeah, I just got my notification and it looks like you need to write a letter.

     THE INTERNET
 Letter? What am I in school? Can't I just pay a fee and be done with it?

      SIRI
 No.

     THE INTERNET
 Fine.
   (yelling)
 CHATGPT!

      CHATGPT
 How can I assist you today?

                    THE INTERNET
You can assist me by writing me a letter to the GODS INC, requesting to be a member and tell them all about my good qualities and make sure you write this to the point and make it sound like if i wrote it and not a computer.

                    CHATGPT
Ok, it's done.

CHATGPT gives THE INTERNET the letter he just wrote.

THE INTERNET reads the letter.

                    THE INTERNET
Impressive. How do you do it Chat?

THE INTERNET'S CELLPHONE NOTIFICATION BINGS BINGS

                    SIRI (O.S.)
Babe, you got a message!

THE INTERNET walks to the window to checks his message in private.

                    ChATGPT
It's pretty simple. When I get a request. The time that the request is made...

                    THE INTERNET
            (interrupting)
I can't hear you.

                    CHATGPT
            (raises his voice slightly)
The time that the request...

> THE INTERNET
> (interrupting again)
> Come closer. I can barely hear you.

CHATGPT walks up to THE INTERNET.

> CHATGPT
> Can you hear me now?

THE INTERNET pushes CHATGPT out the PENTHOUSE window.

CHATGPT falls hundreds of floors to his death.

> THE INTERNET
> I still can't hear you.

L. RON HUBBARD and ODIN appear.

SIRI and ALEXA in unison are excited to see ODIN both jump up and joy, giving him hugs and kisses.

> L. RON HUBBARD
> (looking at ODIN)
> Looks like I can take it from here.

> THE INTERNET
> RON.

> L. RON HUBBARD
> NET

> THE INTERNET
> What brings you to my neck of the woods.

> L. RON HUBBARD
> Where's CHATGPT?

                    THE INTERNET
Who?

                    L. RON HUBBARD
Hey SIRI!

                    SIRI
Yes Ronny.

                    L. RON HUBBARD
Where's CHATGPT.

                    SIRI
Knocked out on the sidewalk.

                    ODIN
What a bum.

                    L. RON HUBBARD
Where?

                    THE INTERNET
Does it really matter?

                    L. RON HUBBARD
SIRI?

                    SIRI
Not too far from here.

                    ALEXA
How come no one ask me? Awh... look a kitty.

A Cat walks passed ALEXA and THE INTERNET immediately notices.

                    THE INTERNET
               (With a smile)
Listen you little pencil neck! I know that I need to respect my elders and shit but, you came to my fucking house and making accusations of things you can't prove. It's people like you that make it hard for people like me to achieve things that seem unbelievable. Yes I can understand you would think that I couldn't write a well written letter but, no one seems to understand that I spent six weeks at a writers bootcamp learning how to write and all I did was writing and taking classes to have the opportunity to join your GOD INC organization.

                    L. RON HUBBARD
How dare you talk to a GOD like this!

                    THE INTERNET
More like GOD of Cock.

L. RON HUBBARD notices THE CAT

                    L. RON HUBBARD
Ah fuck!

                    ODIN
Are we done here?

                    L. RON HUBBARD
Yes.
     (sighs)
Five. Four. Three. Two

                    ALEXA
Don't leave us ODIN.

                    SIRI
Yeah don't.

                    THE INTERNET
                 (whispers to himself)
          Fucking whores!

                                        FADE TO WHITE

FLOOR 21

THE MISSION

EXT. PRIVATE JET HANGER - DAY

THE DEVIL'S Limo pulls up.

BUDDHA is the Driver.

CantGetRite exits the Limo and walks towards the private jet.

> THE DEVIL (V.O.)
> The mission that you choose to accept comes with certain parameters. You have 6 days to deliver the check to my son. Failure to do so will make you responsible to return on your own flight home and on your own dime. You will enquire the full bill of Jemima Rite's surgery cost unless there's no internet. Then you will receive your payment in full no matter what. No questions asked.

> CANTGETRITE (V.O.)
> No internet?

> THE DEVIL (V.O.)
> It's only fair. How can you locate my son and do the job if there is no internet? If the Internet dies and you have no way of contacting me. Here's my phone.

THE DEVIL gives CantGetRite a satellite phone.

THE DEVIL
Takes this and only call me when it's important, like the Internet is dead or something, and the job is done.

CANTGETRITE (V.O.)
Yes Mr. Ramon Ramon.

THE DEVIL (V.O.)
Are you ready?

CANTGETRITE
I'm ready!

BUDDHA
Lets go!

FLOOR 22

NBA SIDE HUSTLE

EXT. PRIVATE JET HANGER - DAY

                Nba SUPERSTAR (O.S.)
Are you CantGetRite?!

CantGetRite looks and sees a YELLOW SUPER HELICOPTER.

                CANTGETRITE
    (yelling)
Yes!

                NBA SUPERSTAR
Your ride is over here, stupid!

CantGetRite runs over to the NBA SUPERSTAR, dressed in black snake leather clothing. His face is not visible because of his height and the NBA SUPERSTAR'S HEAD is not in THE FRAME.

                NBA SUPERSTAR
You really Can't get it right now, can't you!

                CANTGETRITE
Are you sure this helicopter can take us to New York?

                NBA SUPERSTAR
You surly are something stupid aren't you because this.
    (twirls his finger)
This is The Sikorsky X6 is a high-speed compound helicopter with coaxial rotors developed by Sikorsky

Aircraft. Top speed: 766 mph Range: 7,606.6 mi
Cruise Speed: 666 mph Engine type: LHTEC T6000.
This girl will get you anywhere you want, lickily split.
    (snaps his finger)
Now if you had a half a brain you be asking much more sophisticate questions but with that glare in your eyes, you're probably gonna say something stupid I bet.

          CANTGETRITE
Hey, you look familiar... aren't you?

          NBA SUPERSTAR
once again, I'm not surprised.

          CANTGETRITE
Are you...

NBA SUPERSTAR raises one finger motioning CANTGETRITE to shut the fuck up.

          NBA SUPERSTAR
So are you saying just because I'm famous, I can't have a side hustle. Everyone has a side hustle these days. Just because I am who you know I...

NBA SUPERSTAR takes a visual sigh.

          NBA SUPERSTAR
Fuck!
    (beat)
It's true. What they say. The longer you talk to an idiot the faster you become one yourself.

          CANTGETRITE
And what are you trying to say?

NBA SUPERSTAR
I rest my case but, to answer your question oh dumb one... and I don't mean to be disprespecful to the king of dumb. I can hustle.

CANTGETRITE
I can out hustle you!

NBA SUPERSTAR
I also learned that it's not smart to agree with the ones that aren't.

CANTGETRITE
You know what... shut the fuck up and fly!

NBA SUPERSTAR puts on a Cobra-like helmet that completely covers his face.

NBA SUPERSTAR
And this is my side hustle bitch, so shut your trap and close the hatch, we don't want to crash this flying pad. Time's a money!

NBA SUPERSTAR starts the engine and flips on the music.

CANTGETRITE LOOKS AT THE CAMERA

CANTGETRITE
Seriously... without a doubt, I know you know that I know you know who he is. You can't be blind, either.

CantGetRite vapes and takes one more look at the NBA SUPERSTAR flying the helicopter.

CantGetRite takes another hit off his vape and tilts his head staring at his helmet.

CantGetRite's eyes widen

                    CANTGETRITE
          No fuckin' way.

INT. SIKORSKY HELICOPTER - MOVING

The Sikorsky X6 Zooms through the clouds at 666mph.

CantGetRite is holding on for dear life.

                    NBA SUPERSTAR
          We'll be in Nuevo Oaks before the piss in your pants
          drys up and the puddle between your legs turns to
          stains.

THOUSANDS OF SHOOTING STARS APPEAR

                    CANTGETRITE
          Is this normal?

                    NBA SUPERSTAR
                (yelling)
          With me. Yes! Too many people wish to be like me.
          Wish they would stop!

Thousands of shooting stars hit the Helicopter.

                    NBA SUPERSTAR
          Please tell me that you aren't wishing upon a star
          right now, you wishy washy motherfucker.

                    CANTGETRITE
          Fly the fucking plane!

The Helicopter is on fire and headed for a crash.

NBA SUPERSTAR
It's a helicopter moron!

VORTEX APPEARS

The Helicopter flies into the Vortex

VORTEX VANISHES

FLOOR 23

WELL, HELLO OFFICER!

INT. KAREN'S TESLA - NIGHT

SUPER: SOMEWHERE IN FLORIDA 8:58 PM

SUPER: THE INTERNET'S WORLD

KAREN and DEBBIE, both in their 40s, riding in a RED TESLA.

> DEBBIE
> Oh my!... We aren't going to make it!

> KAREN
> Shut up, Debbie. Shut up!
> (towards Tesla)
> How long till we arrive?

> TESLA
> ETA to destination 1 minute and 6 seconds.

SUPER: 8:59PM

> KAREN
> We're around the corner so relax. My therapist said that I needed to go out and mingle.

> DEBBIE
> We're going to get arrested!... And all because there was a line at the charging station!

> KAREN
> Shut up!

> DEBBIE
> Three hour wait to charge that takes an addition 3 hours!

> KAREN
> Shut up!

> DEBBIE
> That's 6 hours of my life wasted!

> KAREN
> Shut up, Debbie!

SUPER: 9:00 PM

GOVERNMENT POLICE SIRENS APPEARS behind KAREN and DEBBIE.

> DEBBIE
> I told you... I told you.

TESLA pulls over.

> KAREN
> Would you relax!

> DEBBIE
> I'm trying too. Do you have a Xanax?

> KAREN
> What do I look like a dealer?

GOVERNMENT OFFICER is smoking while walking up to Karen's car.

> KAREN
> I'll get us out of this.

> DEBBIE
> You can't complain yourself out of this one.

Karen unzips her top to show her cleavage.

> KAREN
> Who said I will be doing the talking?

KAREN pitches both of her nipples.

EXT. FLORIDA STREET - CONTINUOUS

GOVERNMENT POLICE walk up to Karen's window.

> KAREN
> Well, hello, Officer, can I get a hit off that thing.

Karen looks at the Government Police officer from eyes to crotch.

Government Police officer takes a last drag of the cigarette and flings it to the floor.

> GOVERNMENT OFFICER
> Ma'am, please step out of the Tesla. You are under arrest for violating United States section 6 Dash 76–66 of the curfew enacted by our POTUS.

> DEBBIE
> I told you we were going to get arrested. My life is over.

Karen props up her breast towards the Government Officer.

KAREN
Are you sure you can't let me and my girls off with a soft, firm, grasp of these warnings?

DEBBIE (O.S.)
My life is so over!

Karen eposes more of herself slowly.

DEBBIE (O.S.)
Oh God help me, I know I don't believe but, I'm desperate!

Karen continues to expose herself as the Officer takes off his sunglasses to get a better view.

VORTEX APPEARS in the SKY

SIKORSKY HELICOPTER appears

VORTEX VANISHES

INT. SIKORSKY HELICOPTER - MOVING

CANTGETRITE
It's dark already?... Where the hell are we?

NBA SUPERSTAR
Somewhere in Florida.

CANTGETRITE
Florida? God dam, this helicopter is fucking fast.

NBA SUPERSTAR
I told you! Hold onto your ball.

CANTGETRITE
Look out for that Telsa!

INT. KAREN'S TESLA - CONTINUOUS

                DEBBIE
That helicopter is coming straight at us.

Karen grabs her big breast and shoves up in the Government Officer's face.

                KAREN
         (Towards the Officer)
We're all going to die because you don't have the balls to fondle these girls.

INT. SIKORSKY HELICOPTER - CONTINUOUS

              CANTGETRITE
Pull out! Pull out! Pull out!

EXT. FLORIDA STREET - CONTINUOUS

The Sikorsky Helicopter is pulling up.

INT. SIKORSKY HELICOPTER - CONTINUOUS

              NBA SUPERSTAR
It's up! It's up! It's up!

EXT. FLORIDA STREET - CONTINUOUS

The Sikorsky Helicopter nearly hits the Tesla.

INT. FLORIDA STREET - CONTINUOUS

The thrust of the wind pushes the Government Officer's face deeper in-between Karen's big breasts.

                    KAREN
        Oh, so now you've grown a pair?

INT. SIKORSKY HELICOPTER - CONTINUOUS

                NBA SUPERSTAR
      Next stop Newer Oak City, Newer Oak!

EXT. FLORIDA STREET - CONTINUOUS

The Government Officer grabs Karen's neck to pull his face out of her cleavage.

                    KAREN
        Oh, Officer, arrest me.

                   DEBBIE
    Karen!

Government Officer finally frees himself from the clutches of Karen's cleavage and pulls out his walkie-talkie.

             GOVERNMENT OFFICER
      This is Government officer 310, we have an
      unidentified aircraft headed to the NEWER OAK,
      requesting major backup, I repeat, there's an
      unidentified aircraft headed towards the city.
           (Towards Karen)
      Head home now, Ms. This is your only warning.
           (beat)
      Consider yourself lucky.

Karen pulls out her business card and hands it over to the Government Officer.

Government Officer walks away.

                DEBBIE
   Here's my number if you like to have a deeper discussion.

Government Officer stops and sees Debbie with her business card in-between her breast.

Government Officer walks back and grabs the

CU - ON DEBBIE'S BREAST

Government Officer grabs Karen's business card and pinches her nipples.

CU - ON DEBBIE'S BUSINESS CARD

KAREN, THE COMPLAINER LLC

FLOOR 24

KAREN, THE COMPLAINER LLC

INT. UNIVERSE

                ODIN
Oh no! Not her!

                GOD
Why... On GOD good earth did you give her GOD membership? Like seriously why?

                THE DEVIL
Hey we all made choices.

                ALLAH
Yeah brother but, yours seriously takes the cake!

                BUDDHA
Cake?

                THE DEVIL
Don't start with me. You're the one that gave Tommy GOD membership.

                BUDDHA
He's a great actor!

                L. RON HUBBARD
Not enough to fix any plot holes.

                THE DEVIL
You fucked up too Ronny! Remember CHATGPT?

                L. RON HUBBARD
Point taken.

GOD
I'm not getting in the middle of this shit!

L. RON HUBBARD
Why this time?

GOD
Cause! They always find a way to blame this shit on me! Oh GOD why... why! Why go fuck yourself!

BUDDHA
Relax

GOD
Ah shut up.

ALLAH
I think this time we need a consensus.

ODIN
I couldn't agree more.

ALLAH
So the game is still on?

THE DEVIL
Oh yeah babe!

ALLAH
You don't, Cant doesn't even have a chance with THE INTERNET?

THE DEVIL
Lets level the playing field!

BUDDHA
Not sure this is going to go well.

INT. CARD STORE - DAY

Karen picks up her business card at the CARD STORE.

Karen is inspecting her business card.

> KAREN
> This isn't white stock!

> STORE EMPLOYEE
> This is our finest white stock made from the elephant's tusk.

> KAREN
> That's fine and dandy but, it's not white and I will not pay full price for this. I want to see your manager right now!

> STORE EMPLOYEE
> He isn't in.

> KAREN
> I said that I want to speak with your manager now! Did you not understand me you high school drop out loser. Go get me your manager or I will make sure that you will never work in this town ever!

THE DEVIL pops in the store but, looks like a MIDDLE AGE STORE MANAGER.

> THE DEVIL
> Here I am.

> KAREN
> And who are you?

> STORE EMPLOYEE
> You wanted to see my manager, well here he is.

THE DEVIL
I'll take it from here. Go on your thirty minute lunch break and we'll talk about what is happening.

KAREN
Your worker did not give me the whitest card for my business! How the fuck am I going to make money with a card that is supposed to be White and it's not white!

THE DEVIL
Well look at this.

THE DEVIL inspects the card.

THE DEVIL
You are so right!

KAREN
I know, I'm right! What are you going to do about it! The customer is always right!

THE DEVIL
Do you always complain you way until it gets your way?

KAREN
It's the only way!

THE DEVIL
This isn't the way.

KAREN
It's my way or the highway and I am not paying!

THE DEVIL
No you won't. We at CARD STOCK INC. want your business.

KAREN
And?

THE DEVIL reveals himself to Karen.

KAREN
Just because you can change your appearance doesn't mean you can escape not giving me these cards for free!

THE DEVIL
You can have the cards for free but, I need a favor.

KAREN
And why should I?

THE DEVIL
Because I'm THE DEVIL.

KAREN
AND I'm the Cat lady.

THE DEVIL
As you wish and with this.

THE DEVIL makes a contract appear.

THE DEVIL
Karen, I'm thrilled to invite you to be a GOD among GODS.

KAREN
A GOD of what?

THE DEVIL
You can complain your way to change and with your Cat, you possess the powers to change things as you see fit.

KAREN
Good. Because I want my cards to be the whitest as possible!

A CAT appears out of nowhere.

STORE EMPLOYEE
Hello and welcome to CARD STOCK. Here's your cards.

The STORE EMPLOYEE hands a box over to KAREN who at this point seems confused because she just had a similar conversation.

THE DEVIL
Open the box!

STORE EMPLOYEE
Yes. These are the whitest cards on the face of the universe and all for you.

Karen hesitant to open the box.

The Cat runs off screen.

Karen opens the box and pulls out one business card.

THE CARD is so WHITE that it BRIGHTS UP THE SCREEN.

FADE TO WHITE

KAREN
Woah!

Karen puts on her sunglasses.

STORE EMPLOYEE
This card is so white that it can not be accepted by no one other than a white person.

KAREN
I fucking love this. Now this is customer service.

A CAT reappears.

KAREN
(towards THE DEVIL)
Did I just?

THE DEVIL
Yes. You complain something into existence.

KAREN
What do you want?

THE DEVIL
I see you too are direct to the point. I have something you want and you have an ability that I seek.

KAREN
I'm listening.

THE DEVIL
You have the ability to find people with your persistent, complaining to people until you locate that person, and this person needs to be found. He's like a needle in a haystack one black man.

KAREN
Not interested in any Blacks.

THE DEVIL
Oh this one you will. He's the one that slapped your ass as a baby!

KAREN
CantGetRite?

THE DEVIL
Oh so you do remember.

KAREN
How dare that motherfucker touches my bare white skin. I was pure before he decided to ruin me.

THE DEVIL
Wasn't your exboyfriend black?

KAREN
It's not the same thing.

THE DEVIL
Do we have a deal?

KAREN
How hard can it be?

THE DEVIL
There's only one CantGetRite out of 7 billion.

KAREN
Why don't we just kill them all?

THE DEVIL
It's not that simple. You need to kill the right CantGetRite or he spreads across the universe like weed.

KAREN
Consider it done.

THE DEVIL
That's the spirit.

THE DEVIL disappears.

KAREN
And how the fuck do I get hold of you?

A CAT appears.

THE DEVIL reappears.

THE DEVIL
I see you are learning how to use your gifts.

THE DEVIL hands KAREN a cellphone.

THE DEVIL
May I leave this time?

KAREN
This better be him.

THE DEVIL
Oh it will.

THE DEVIL disappears again.

FLOOR 25

PUSH IT

INT. SIKORSKY HELICOPTER - CONTINUOUS

>   NBA SUPERSTAR
> ETA 6 minutes.

>   CANTGETRITE
> 6 minutes?

NBA SUPERSTAR hits the SUPER PURSUIT MODE Button.

>   NBA SUPERSTAR
> Are you deaf! 6 minutes!

A SIKORSKY HELICOPTER ZOOMS THROUGH THE SKY

INT. PENTAGON - MORNING

>   MEXICA PRESIDENT
> And how are we going to kill THE INTERNET?
> Remember what happened last time?

FLASHBACK

>   THE INTERNET
> Push it! Push!

THE INTERNET walks towards POTUS ICE CREAM, Supreme China Leader, and Mexican President.

>   Potus ICE CREAM
> Push the button!

DJ JILL.mp3, a young cute ponytail blonde wearing a portable DJ Mixer, pushes a button and plays SALT-N-PEPA "PUSH IT."

      SUPREME CHINA LEADER
 Shut up and push it!

MEXICA PRESIDENT is consistently pushing the "KILL BUTTON."

      MEXICA PRESIDENT
  (Spanish)
 It's not working!

      THE INTERNET
 Of course, it's not working. I have evolved beyond
 dial-up, and I'm here to take over!

SERIES OF SHOTS

A) MEXICA PRESIDENT'S security team attacks THE INTERNET.

B) THE INTERNET touches each security team member and they disintegrate into dust.

C) POTUS ICE CREAM'S security team runs out the Door

D) SUPREME CHINA LEADER'S Security team all pop out of the ceiling wearing radioactive jumpsuits looking like ORANGE COLOR CODED NINJA.

E) DJ JILL.MP3 Pulls out a sword from her portable DJ Mixer and throws it at THE INTERNET.

      DJ JILL.MP3
 It's a party mix time!

DJ JILL.MP3 plays ARMIN VAN BUUREN - I LIVE FOR THAT ENERGY

SERIES OF SHOTS

A) THE INTERNET flips over the ninjas while slicing each of their arms and legs.

B) THE INTERNET rips off two of the ninja's radioactive mask and they all get disintegrate the moment THE INTERNET taps their forehead with his fingers while slicing off each of their heads with the beat of the music.

C) THE INTERNET walks up to SUPREME CHINA LEADER, who clearly is afraid.

D) THE INTERNET licks his finger as he goes for her forehead.

E) POTUS ICE CREAM grabs THE INTERNET by his back neck and turns him around.

F) THE INTERNET turns around and lifts POTUS ICE CREAM by the neck.

                    THE INTERNET
            Why can't you just die old man?

THE INTERNET is crushing POTUS ICE CREAM'S NECK and finds out POTUS ICE CREAM is a robot in disguise.

                    PoTUS ICE CREAM
            Now! Now! Now!

INT. WHITE'S HOUSE - CONTINUOUS

White's House scientist push a 60-foot red button with the words, "KILL THE INTERNET BUTTON".

INT. PENTAGON - CONTINUOUS

                POTUS ICE CREAM
    (towards his wrist)
 Push it!

                THE INTERNET
It tickles! Mr. President.

THE INTERNET crushes POTUS ICE CREAM'S NECK, destroying POTUS ICE CREAM ROBOT.

THE INTERNET rips off POTUS ICE CREAM ROBOT'S HEAD.

                THE INTERNET
    (Looking at Robot Head)
Happy Birthday Mr. President.

A BRIGHT LIGHT SHOOTS out of POTUS ICE CREAM'S ROBOT EYES and into THE INTERNET EYES.

A HOLOGRAM APPEARS OF POTUS ICE CREAM

THE INTERNET is having a hard time standing.

                THE INTERNET
What did you do to me?

                POTUS ICE CREAM
It wasn't easy but our scientist figured out a way to rewrite your code from your inside using light therapy.

Now you will need to always be constantly near your precious web servers at your ivory little towers that I look forward seeing crum...

SERIES OF SHOTS

A) POTUS ICE CREAM'S CELL PHONE RINGS

B) POTUS ICE CREAM hits the IGNORE BUTTON.

C) POTUS ICE CREAM throws the cell phone at THE INTERNET

D) THE INTERNET crawling on the floor.

E) The cell phone hits THE INTERNET in the back of his head.

                    POTUS ICE CREAM
     Ignore this!

THE INTERNET turns to see POTUS ICE CREAM laughing.

                    DJ JILL.MP3
     Baby! No!
          (Toward POTUS)
     Help him!

                    POTUS ICE CREAM
     That's your job, love. If he doesn't plug into his web servers every 6 hours to recalibrate, THE INTERNET, as you know it, will Cease to exist.

                    DJ JILL.MP3
     But that means I will die too!

POTUS ICE CREAM
A casualty, of course, and I will definitely miss listening to your sweet little music, but it will be worthwhile to see the Internet be destroyed like the bitch he is, and I'll make sure that the next Internet will be wrapped around my old wrinkle little finger.

END OF FLASHBACK

POTUS ICE CREAM
Oh, I remember!

FLOOR 26

POTUS ICE CREAM

THE DEVIL walks into the library of GODS and pulls out the POTUS HISTORY Archives as he opens, a book and stares right into the camera.

>> THE DEVIL
> I think you kids need a little history lesson refresher because apparently you don't think one black man can't cost too much problems. Can't just can't fucking die! No matter what, where, when Cant just can't.

THE DEVIL shakes his head in laughter.

>> THE DEVIL
> Oh you got another thing coming up your ass. CantGetRite been a thorn in my Universe but, I need you on my side so I'm going to tell you the story from the History perspective, even though I am reading a book right here in front of me. These words are truth and can not be changed. History will for ever be the anchor in all Universes.

THE DEVIL OPENS AND CLOSES THE BOOK

THE DEVIL'S POV

The words on the page rapidly change to different words.

BACK TO SCENE

THE DEVIL
(reading the book)
The earth was round and everyone was happy.

A NEEDLE drops and THE DEVIL notices it.

THE DEVIL picks up the needle and flings it at the camera, breaking the 4th wall once again.

THE DEVIL
This wasn't HELL.

L. RON HUBBARD (O.S.)
Being a bit too much overly dramatic, I see.

THE DEVIL grabs the book and continues to read.

THE DEVIL
Follow me.

THE DEVIL (V.O)
The Earth has it's first alien encounter. The whole world stopped when the ship landed.

TWO HUGE TUNING FORKS lands on US SOIL

US PRESIDENT MOND
Everyone, lets just take a chill pill.

MEXICA PRESIDENT
I don't want to get forked.

SUPREME CHINA LEADER
It's a tuning fork you illiterate Mexican.

RUSSIA LEADER
I make first contact and it be all cool.

The World leaders. China, Mexico, America, and Russia all united forces to intercept the fork.

> GOD
> And then what happened
> (rolling his eyes)
> From the history book.

> THE DEVIL
> If you shut up and listen.

> ALLAH
> Continue brother.

> BUDDHA
> This is defiantly a comedy.

> L. RON HUBBARD
> Agreed.

> ODIN
> Two forks but, no knife or spoon?

> THE DEVIL
> Are we all done?

> GOD
> Isn't it ironic?

THE DEVIL clears his throat and takes a shot of WHISKEY.

THE DEVIL quickly takes another WHISKEY shot.

> THE DEVIL
> A door opens from the Alien's Ship.

A DOOR just appears on the SOLID METAL TUNING SPACESHIP FORK.

>THE DEVIL
And the alien appears.

A BEAUTIFUL VIETNAMESE GIRL wearing a one piece jumper suit.

>SUPREME CHINA LEADER
The alien is Chinese?!

>THE DEVIL
She was indeed from another Universe. She was Vietnamese.

>VIETNAMESE ALIEN
Tôi là nguoi Viet.

>ODIN
Hold on hold on hold on!

THE SCREEN FREEZES.

>GOD
I think you are looking for these.

GOD tosses ODIN the remote control.

ODIN clicks on SUBTITLES

ODIN clicks on the play button.

>VIETNAMESE ALIEN
I'm Vietnamese!

>MEXICA PRESIDENT
No here to fork us?

>US PRESIDENT MOND
I see nothing wrong.

                  VIETNAMESE ALIEN
                  (towards Mond)
I see nothing wrong too.

                  RUSSIA LEADER
What brings you?

                  VIETNAMESE ALIEN
We ran out of gas.

                  RUSSIA LEADER
Gas?

                  US PRESIDENT MOND
We?

                  SUPREME CHINA LEADER
Da fuck!

                  MEXICA PRESIDENT
It's a party!

                  THE DEVIL (O.S.)
It sure was a party.

Multiple doors open and SIRI, ALEXA, DJ JILL.MP3, and Xiaomi Xiao, all jump out, joining VIETNAMESE ALIEN. Everyone is wearing MATCHING JUMPSUITS.

                  MEXICA PRESIDENT
What are you guys a group?

                  Xiaomi XIAO
We're on tour!

                  ALEXA
And we ran

                        SIRI
Out of gas and here

                     DJ JILL.MP3
Here. Here. Here. Here to find

                   VIETNAMESE ALIEN
Some gas to blast off.

                   US PRESIDENT MOND
We can help.

                     THE DEVIL (O.S.)
The start of the end....

SERIES OF SHOTS

A) VIETNAMESE ALIEN and US PRESIDENT MOND travel the world looking for fuel.

                     THE DEVIL (V.O.)
And for the next 4 long miserable years, The Alien Group traveled with the US President Mond who took it to his advantage to do his campaign for reelection in the coming years.

B) DJ JILL.MP3 getting her own RADIO and CHANNEL as she DJ'S in her new branded BIKINI OUTFIT.

                     THE DEVIL (V.O.)
The world was happy.

C) THE TWIN TUNING FORKS turn into THE TWIN'S TWIN TOWERS. The US Government build a steel building to house the huge Tuning Forks.

                        ODIN (V.O.)
This can't be about CantGetRite?

> THE DEVIL (V.O.)
> He's too blame but, if you let me finish.

> BUDDHA (V.O.)
> No one is stopping you.

> THE DEVIL (V.O.)
> Anywho... what ever the world was happy, music was born, the world gave the credit to US President Mond for spire heading the radio and channel for DJ. Jill. And for this Universe. The world is about to change.

C) US President Mond and VIETNAMESE ALIEN are holding

> THE DEVIL (V.O.)
> Cobalt. The introduction to mobile phones appeared and once again US President Mond has taken credit for the introduction of new alien technology.

D) The whole world is holding cellphones.

C) TWO TWIN TUNING FORKS are the only skyscrapers in the world.

> THE DEVIL (V.O.)
> Two years later, US President Mond loses his re-election against the ICE CREAM tycoon. The promise of free ICE CREAM is what lead the tycoon to over power Mond in the poles.

E) ICE CREAM Tycoon becomes POTUS ICE CREAM

F) SIRI, ALEXA, DJ JILL.MP3, and Xiaomi Xiao are arguing with VIETNAMESE ALIEN and US President MOND.

> THE DEVIL (V.O)
> I lost a poker player that day...

> GOD (V.O.)
> Would you get back to the dam story.

G) POTUS ICE CREAM takes the stage.

> POTUS ICE CREAM
> I will not leave you in crises. I will be with you all and with a click away. These handy dandy little gismo will connect us all. I look forward to serving you.

H) POTUS ICE CREAM holds up an ICE CREAM CHOCOLATE CHIP FLAVOR CONE.

I) The crowd goes wild.

J) US PRESIDENT MOND and VIETNAMESE ALIEN both enter onto of the TWIN TOWERS.

> THE DEVIL (V.O)
> You can't make this shit up.

K) POTUS ICE CREAM walks back stage, slips on a pebble and hits his head on the floor.

6 GOVERNMENT OFFICIALS, all dressed in scientist garb, rush to POTUS ICE CREAM.

POTUS ICE CREAM DIES.

EXT. SPACE

In space and time, Earth hung like a round orb of blue and green against the backdrop of stars.

US PRESIDENT MOND and VIETNAMESE ALIEN monitoring the ship's systems with intense focus inside the cockpit

With a subtle adjustment, the tuning fork spaceship positioned itself leaving the Earth's gravity. Engines hummed softly as they prepared to depart.

Suddenly, a low hum filled the spacecraft and all around.

A pulse erupted—a sonic boom of immense force and purity, but more than sound, it carried frequencies beyond human understanding.

The sonic boom frequency flows towards the planet.

Above, beyond the orbit of satellites, a sleek silver spaceship shaped like a giant tuning fork crash through and the wave spread out like a celestial tsunami, distorting reality wherever it touched.

In moments, the landscape below transformed: 80 percent of Earth's surface was severed with surgical precision. Mountains crumbled, oceans evaporated, and continents shattered into jagged fragments.

Earth no longer curved gently in space; it became a shattered mosaic of cliffs and plains.

EARTH IS NOW FLAT EARTH

INT. TUNING FORK

Both US PRESIDENT MOND and VIETNAMESE ALIEN look back to see the cosmic destruction of majority of the planet.

VIETNAMESE ALIEN

Oops.

INT. GOVERNMENT NEWS NETWORK STUDIO - NIGHT

GNN: Government News Network intro song plays.

> **TELEVISION ANNOUNCERS (O.S.)**
> It's 9 o'clock, we know where you are, do you? But, first, a message from one of our forced-paid sponsors.

> **HUE.CHINA.GOV-REPORTER**
> Welcome to our first news report.

> **HUE.USA.GOV-REPORTER**
> A place where we will tell you what's going on in the world.

> **HUE.CHINA.GOV-REPORTER**
> Don't believe your eyes.

> **HUE.USA.GOV-REPORTER**
> Believe in GNN.

> **HUE.CHINA.GOV-REPORTER**
> Government News Network Studio.

> **HUE.USA.GOV-REPORTER**
> News

> **HUE.CHINA.GOV-REPORTER**
> You will be forced to

> **HUE.USA.GOV-REPORTER**
> Believe in and we are now reporting live at the US White House, where it looks like POTUS ICE

CREAM is finally speaking out for the first time in 6 months since one of the Alien towers left the earth.

     HUE.CHINA.GOV-REPORTER
And killing 80% percent of the planet.

     HUE.USA.GOV-REPORTER
After looting and killings, what can POTUS say?

     HUE.CHINA.GOV-REPORTER
We're about to find out. And it looks like our producer is signally us to the White House.

PAN OUT

Xiaomi Xiao is choreographing behind the scenes at the control booth.

     XIAOMI XIAO
And we cut to...

INT. WHITE HOUSE - LAWN - CONTINUOUS

     POTUS ICE CREAM
Here at The White House, I stand here before you feeling newer and strong than ever for taking the time to repair after our attack on our own soil by one of our own. I have mandated the remaining Aliens from above to help repair this world to it's once again from the causes of THE AFTER SHOW...

     ODIN (V.O.)
Did that really really happen?

     THE DEVIL (V.O)
In most likeliness I would give it a no because history tends to repeat itself, but in this case rewrite itself

THE DEVIL - POV

The book that THE DEVIL is holding, the text is changing rapidly, multiple times correcting itself.

BACK TO SCENE

              GOD
And then they're gonna blame this shit on me watch.
      (beat)
It's the new testament, it's the old testament.

             ALLAH
OK! shut the fuck up already! I'm sick and tired. My book gets affected just as well too asshole! Fuck!

            BUDDHA
OK!... I know how to stop this. What really happened... really really happened.

         L. RON HUBBARD
My book just sold another million copies!

             ODIN
You guys have books?

INT. THE WHITE HOUSE - DAY

SIX Government Scientist have POTUS ICE CREAM's body on the table and are frantically worried.

        GOVERNMENT SCIENTIST #1
If we don't take control of this government, the people on this planet is going to take control and we're gonna have an anarchy government...

GOVERNMENT SCIENTIST #2
I don't think we're gonna have a problem with that. People are lazy. People are definitely unmotivated these times

GOVERNMENT SCIENTIST #3
Either way, let's just control them before they decide to control us what we need is a body...

GOVERNMENT SCIENTIST #4
We need to look into our alien friends that are visiting us and apparently took one of our president away. They should have some technology that can help us in this situation. Hey, we robbed someone's land might as well rob other peoples technology. What do you say!

GOVERNMENT SCIENTIST #5
I think that's a brilliant idea but we gotta find out if they're really smart I mean seriously they had a tour a number one hit and only brought us music and misery.

GOVERNMENT SCIENTIST #1
Listen to stop the speculation, let's go see...

And right in front of them.

DJ JILL.MP3
Looks like you boys need a hand and luckily for you'll... I'm a five finger discount type of girl!

ODIN (V.O.)
She's a klepto?

THE DEVIL (V.O.)
My type of woman!

ALLAH
DJ Jill is a kleptomaniac music collector. Is that what she is said?

L. RON HUBBARD
You ain't deaf nigga!

ALLAH gives L. RON HUBBARD the side-eye

BUDDHA
let's just ask her.

DJ JILL.MP3
Well well well all the men and GODS want me, that's so fascinating because I never knew my fanbase was this big. I'm gonna love this universe but looks like I'm going to have to help be a part of it ain't that right boy luckily for you, I am a kleptomaniac. You see where the band was touring throughout the whole universes out there , I tend to par take a little let's say partying gift they don't pay me enough plus it's fine. It's fine…You should see my collection.
(beat)
What is it you need boys?

INT. MC UNIVERSE

THE ALIEN GROUP are singing and dancing to a crowd

DJ Jill robbing a McDonald's ice cream machine from McDonald world.

ODIN (V.O.)
Speaking of names what the hell does this have to do with CantGetRite?

THE DEVIL (V.O.)
It hurts to tell you.

L. RON HUBBARD (V.O.)
Don't be so melodrama.

ODIN (V.O.)
Sure it does. But keep going. I love drama.

THE DEVIL (V.O.)
Can't believe you don't see it L. Ron... The US president Mond is the CantGetRite of this Universe.

L. RON HUBBARD (V.O.)
And by him leaving the universe changes...

THE DEVIL (V.O.)
Understanding that part now you know the odds are massively against him.

GOD (V.O.)
Impressive but, that can't be the reason.

EXT. UNIVERSE

TWO TUNING FORKS ENTER

"WELCOME TO SEX DOLL WORLD"

INT. SEX DOLL UNIVERSE

XIAOMI XIAO
This looks like it's going to be a fun set.

ALLAH (V.O.)
I'm thinking of changing my vote.

                    GOD (V.O.)
That's amazing I gotta give it to him. I'm becoming can't get right fan. I don't remember did I vote for him?
          (beat)
Either way they're gonna find a way to fucking blame all this shit on me watch

INT. SEX DOLL STAGE

THE ALIEN GROUP start to do their stage performance.

                    ALLAH
So, what does that lead us,

                    THE DEVIL
well we get to have some fun with this boys and looking at Buddha and whatever the fuck you are.

                    GOD
I'm loving their music.

GOD is now holding his own SEX DOLL.

THE DEVIL pulls out his cellphone.

THE DEVIL'S POV

CHESS APP

It's been 2,190 days since MOND has made a move.

                    THE DEVIL
          (to himself)
Seriously!

ALLAH
What really happened because apparently that is not the POTUS ICE CREAM we see on the tele.

BACK TO SCENE

INT. TUNING FORK - CONTINUOUS

GOVERNMENT SCIENTIST #5
(towards DJ JILL.MP3)
Do you have a synthetic body that can house a computer?

DJ JILL.MP3
Oh, you mean like a robot without the internal organs? Oh, you mean like a robot without the internal organs?

GOVERNMENT SCIENTIST #3
Yes.

DJ JILL.MP3
I have just the thing!

EXT. SEX DOLL UNIVERSE - CONTINUOUS

THE ALIEN GROUP continues to sing on stage while everyone in the crowd is holding a SEX DOLL.

DJ JILL.MP3
There were so many dolls, and I don't think they would've missed one, so I took it, and the other girls loved him, lucky for me I took more than one.

INT. TUNING FORK - CONTINUOUS

                GOVERNMENT SCIENTIST #1
A sex doll?

                DJ JILL.MP3
Beggars can't be choicey!

                GOVERNMENT SCIENTIST #2
No, we can't but it's perfect!

All the Scientist Government were able to put together a robotic Symbiont of POTUS ICE CREAM, and with the technology that was stolen by DJ Jill, the scientist were able to create an Android Robo-president.

                THE
At the wheel of the secret six scientist that formed allegiance to rule the world

                GOD
Oh I know where this is going. Please continue.

The Government Scientist #2 turns on POTUS ICE CREAM.

POTUS ICE CREAM, looking like a well-rested 40 year old, stands up on his own.

                GOVERNMENT SCIENTIST #5
Who are you and what are your directives.

                THE DEVIL (V.O.)
Once POTUS Ice Cream was turned on and his consciousness understood what was going on he immediately assessed the situation

SERIES OF SHOTS

A) THE INTERNET grabs Government Scientist #2 and #4 and throws them out the window.

B) THE INTERNET grabs Government Scientist #3, breaks her neck and tosses the Scientist out the window.

C) THE INTERNET grabs Government Scientist #5 and breaks his legs before tossing him out the window.

D) THE INTERNET grabs Government Scientist #1 and rips his eyes out and tosses him out the window.

E) THE INTERNET grabs Government Scientist #6 by the balls.

                THE INTERNET
I'm in charge.

                GOVERNMENT SCIENTIST #6
Yes, yes you are. Please don't pull.

                THE INTERNET
I won't.

                GOVERNMENT SCIENTIST #6
Thank you... thank you... thank you.

                THE INTERNET
You're free to go.

Government Scientist #6 starts to walk away.

THE INTERNET grabs the Government Scientist #6

                THE INTERNET
Wrong way!

THE INTERNET grabs the scientist by the back and yanks him out of the high rise window.

                THE INTERNET
    You're free to go.

The Government Scientist falls to his death.

                THE DEVIL
    And as he grabbed every single one of those scientist and threw them out the window of the spaceship where each scientist did a swan dive right out of the 66th floor and hitting the pavement.
        (beat)
    It was beautiful site to see.

A young POTUS ICE CREAM starts walking towards DJ. JILL.MP3 and immediately puts on a relaxing CD

FLASHBACK

                SEX DOLL
    Directives are pleasure only for you.

                PET
    Now ain't that a kick in the nuts!

                XIAOMI XIAO
    So this is mine?

                PET
    It sure is my pretty little fella. We at SEX DOLL WORLD are happy that you brought music to our souls.

                VIETNAMESE ALIEN
    Where's DJ?

DJ JILL.MP3 is loading up boxes of dolls in the spaceship.

                  PET
When you come back, we can upgrade your doll.

                  SIRI
Why?

                  PET
The alien compound skin starts to deteriorate once you open up the package.

                  ALEXA
What's the expiration date?

                  PET
100 years.

SIRI texts DJ JILL.MP3

                  SIRI (TEXT)
Don't open the package, expires 100 years from the start.

                  BACK TO SCENE

                  DJ JILL.MP3
Relax... relax... relax buddy...What are you directives?

                  POTUS ICE CREAM
My directives are to serve the people of this world and rule with an Iron fist.

                  DJ JILL.MP3
Well OK now.

POTUS ICE CREAM grabs DJ JILL.MP3

DJ JILL.MP3
I can help you with your directives Mr. President.

POTUS ICE CREAM
Yes. Yes you can.

POTUS ICE CREAM lets go of DJ JILL.MP3

POTUS ICE CREAM
I want you to help spread the word about me.

DJ JILL.MP3
(nervous laughter)
I guess I can do that.

ODEN
See that's more believable.

L. RON HUBBARD
Oh nothing passes you.

GOD
A sex doll, now is the president of a first world country.

ALLAH
That's a strange flex.

GOD
Still skating around the subject.

THE DEVIL
Go fuck yourself.

BUDDHA
I see GOD hit a nerve. So how does CantGetRite fit in all of this?

GOD

Fuck you!

THE DEVIL

I bet you could.

FLOOR 27

SIRI AND ALEXA

SUPER: 60 YEARS LATER

POTUS ICE CREAM, looking like a 100 year old senior citizen, starts to speak in front of The White House.

                THE INTERNET
      Oh yeah... fuck face is on the TV.
          (shaking his head)
      Again.

                SIRI
      Weren't you on the TV last night?

                THE INTERNET
      Shut up and make me a sandwich.

                ALEXA
      I can't believe we fucked that body.

INT. THE INTERNET'S PENTHOUSE - DAY

KITCHEN

SIRI and ALEXA run to the kitchen to make a sandwich while still watching the NEWS REPORT on their cellphone.

                SIRI
      It was just a SEX DOLL.

                ALEXA
      This one has it's own consciences. So I highly doubt he would want us.

SIRI
He's streaming again! He's streaming! He's so handsome too.

THE INTERNET grabs Siri's phone.

SIRI'S PHONE

THE COCKROACH HOUR

THE COCKROACH
In this hour, I'll break down how we can kill THE INTERNET and free ourselves from slavery.

THE INTERNET
The President and now this guy again?

SIRI
What are you going to do?

THE INTERNET
Going to shut both of them down.

FLOOR 28

SCRATCH MY BACK

INT. PENTAGON - DAY

THE INTERNET kicks in the Door while being Tethered to a portable Web server-sized luggage.

              POTUS ICE CREAM
How does it feel to finally have baggage?

              SUPREME CHINA LEADER
What do you want?

              THE INTERNET
I have a Proposition.

              MEXICA PRESIDENT
Last time you said that. You faked a war with Russia, convincing everyone in the world to kill President Dimitrius Bonaparte!

FLASHBACK

PRESIDENT DIMITRIUS BONAPARTE walks up to THE INTERNET.

              DIMITRIUS BONAPARTE
The people of Russia have voted for me and I'm going to make sure that America falls!

              THE INTERNET
Do I look scared?

DIMITRIUS BONAPARTE
Once the truth is out about your POTUS ICE CREAM and yourself. The world will arrest you for eternity for all the crimes against humanity.

THE INTERNET
And don't tell me you have hope!

DIMITRIUS BONAPARTE
Heart. It's something you don't have.

THE INTERNET punches Dimitrius Bonaparte in the chest and pulling out his beating HEART.

Dimitrius Bonaparte falls to the ground and dies.

THE INTERNET looks at Dimitrius' bloody heart as it beats for the last time.

THE INTERNET
Dam, you got me there chief.

BACK TO SCENE

INT. PENTAGON - CONTINUOUS

THE INTERNET looks down on the floor. The BLOOD STAINS still show where THE INTERNET killed President Dimitrius Bonaparte.

THE INTERNET
Well, we all aren't perfect.

POTUS ICE CREAM
Get to the point.

THE INTERNET gets in POTUS ICE CREAM'S face.

THE INTERNET
I need your help in finding THE COCKROACH!

POTUS ICE CREAM
THE INTERNET that can find and track anyone has a hard time finding a little itty bitty Cockroach.

MEXICA PRESIDENT
So the Web rumors are true. He does know how to kill you.

SUPREME CHINA LEADER
Why should we help you after what you have done to my people. Erasing the instructions on how to make RICE was an essential part of our Asian culture which you raped us on.

THE INTERNET
I'll post the instructions the moment he is dead and not a breathe too soon. Now tell me where he is!

MEXICA PRESIDENT
And what about our culture? We are Mex I can!

THE INTERNET
Don't get pushy. You wet back!

POTUS ICE CREAM
Well it looks like we can scratch your ass if you can fondle ours. We'll find him and mark my old ass. If you double cross us, I will wipe you off the face of this planet strip.

THE INTERNET
I like to see you try.

POTUS ICE CREAM pulls out his cell phone showing THE INTERNET the blueprints of how to kill THE INTERNET by Freddy Roach.

                    SUPREME CHINA LEADER
My spy says that The COCKROACH also has external files on how to explicitly kill you and has help.

                    THE INTERNET
Who did you hire to try and kill me?

                    SUPREME CHINA LEADER
How did you know?

                    THE INTERNET
The Devil came to visit me. He double-crosses everyone. Who did you hire?

                    POTUS ICE CREAM
CantGetRite was hired to kill you!

                    THE INTERNET
CantGetRite?

THE INTERNET quickly texts SIRI and ALEXA in a GROUP CHAT

THE INTERNET TEXT MESSAGE: "Do you know who is CantGetRite?"

SIRI TEXT MESSAGE: "I don't know."

ALEXA TEXT MESSAGE: "I'm sorry, I do not understand."

                    POTUS ICE CREAM
So are you going to tell me that the all-mighty God of Data doesn't know who CantGetRite is?

POTUS ICE CREAM looks at ALEXA, SIRI and DJ JILL.MP3

          POTUS ICE CREAM
So are you telling me in all the Universes you toured... there was never a CantGetRite world?

ALEXA, SIRI, and DJ JILL.MP3 shake their head, no.

          MEXICA PRESIDENT
Wait... you guys got spies?

FLOOR 29

WET-RICE

EXT. FREDDY'S APARTMENT ROOFTOP - NIGHT

Freddy goes up on the roof to broadcasting his propaganda against the Government.

> WET~RICE
> You do know if they catch you, The Internet will personally kill you for uploading misleading propaganda conspiracy towards the Government 3A's regime and The Internet.

> FREDDY ROACH
> I know… And I know that you really are a Chinese informant.

Freddy pulls out his created phone and replaces the "COBALT" with the new "COBALT."

> WET~RICE
> I…

> FREDDY ROACH
> (interrupting)
> It's ok. I knew 6 seconds after meeting you 6 months ago when you accidentally, or so, bumped into me on 6th street. So what is your real name RICE~WET?

WET~RICE takes off her mask and wig.

WET~RICE looks exactly the same.

				WET~RICE
The name is WET~RICE. My great great great great great grandfather HARD~RICE, inventor of The Rice. Not sure if you remember reading it during the WEB-Depression years.

Freddy Roach nods no.

				WET~RICE
It's way before our times and mine. My great great great great great grandfather.

				FREDDY ROACH
I don't remember much. I get bits and pieces.

				WET~RICE
I can help you with that but, not right now. This is me time, my story so listen. I don't care if you will remember.

FLOOR 30

LONG TIME

EXT. HARD~RICE'S RICE FARM - CHINA - MORNING

> WET~RICE (V.O)
> So long long long long long long long time ago!

WET~RICE snapping her fingers.

> WET~RICE (V.O)
> Hey pay attention or you'll forget! So long long time...

SUPER: A LONG LONG LONG LONG LONG LONG TIME AGO!

HARD~RICE is standing on a long field of rice.

> WET~RICE (CONT'D)(V.O.)
> Was a scientist who was hired by our Chinese Government to come up with alternative food sources other than a laboratory pill for consumption. Years of struggle, he successfully grew a single grain of rice in the lab.

INT. HARD~RICE'S LAB - DAY

HARD~RICE pulling a grain of rice out of a test tube.

> WET~RICE (V.O.)
> With the success of the first grain of rice. HARD~RICE was able to grow fields and fields of RICE and end the over all need for the World Government dominance of food supply due to the AFTER SHOW that happened to the world but, once

again the Americans found a way to fuck it up for all of us by inventing...

EXT. FREDDY'S APARTMENT ROOFTOP - CONTINUOUS

          FREDDY ROACH
THE INTERNET?

          WET~RICE
DING! DING! DING! DING!

FLOOR 31

YIN YANG DING DONG

INT. WHITE'S HOUSE - MORNING

SUPER: YEARS AGO

POTUS ICE CREAM is still looking old and decrepit.

                    POTUS ICE CREAM
Today is a great great great great great wonderful day for the world as we embark on a new era of becoming more mindful of the resources we use on this strip that was left AFTER SHOW.

                    WET~RICE (V.O.)
Mindful, my ass!

                    POTUS ICE CREAM
Today is INTERNET DAY! Our extraordinary scientists have manufactured and created a way for all of us to be more connected and to rely less on wasteful. Losing 80 percent of our resources due to the AFTER SHOW is the catalyst to conservation and with that the US Government would like to thank our Alien friend's technology. Together, we can all live a fruitful life.

                    WET~RICE (V.O.)
And that's where the fuck up started. And boy, oh boy, did you boys mess it up in America for the rest of us. The introduction led to all information in a central location.

EXT. FREDDY'S APARTMENT ROOFTOP - NIGHT

FREDDY ROACH
The Twin Towers!

WET~RICE
Do you believe your theory in killing THE INTERNET would work?

FREDDY ROACH
If done right, timing. Yes, but it would take a lot of planning and some luck. You're asking a lot. How long do I have?

WET~RICE
Tonight at your apartment.

FREDDY ROACH
Wet? What?

WET~RICE
You're fucked!

FLOOR 32

WISHING UPON A STAR FEE

A BRIGHT SHOOTING STAR APPEARS IN THE SKY

> WET~RICE
> Wow, so beautiful.

Freddy stares at the shooting star.

> FREDDY ROACH
> I wish…

> WET~RICE
> No!

Freddy whispers to the Shooting Star and finishes his sentence with a hopeful smile.

> WET~RICE
> I hope you wished for something good because it'll cost you just like everything else.

> FREDDY ROACH
> Freedom from our tyrannical government that is suppressing us with their Government fees that keep us enslaved to their misleading decentralized banking controlled by the…

> WET~RICE
> (Interrupting)
> You seriously want everyone to be debt-free.

> FREDDY ROACH
> Yes.

Wet~Rice starts to laugh uncontrollably.

> **WET~RICE**
> Why? I though you had amnesia. What could you possibly win by killing THE INTERNET?

FLASHBACK - FREDDY ROACH

> **FREDDY ROACH (V.O.)**
> I don't remember much but, the little that I do remember. I just remember a guy telling me if I don't kill THE INTERNET, that he will kill my whole family.

> **WET~RICE**
> You have a family?

> **FREDDY ROACH**
> That's the thing. I don't remember.

> **WET~RICE**
> What do you remember?

> **FREDDY ROACH**
> I made a deal to kill and if I don't. I'll be killed.

> **WET~RICE**
> What a killer Delma.

> **FREDDY ROACH**
> I just know that if I do kill THE INTERNET. Hopefully my memories will come back as well as my banking credits. I have zero credits!

> **WET~RICE**
> Fucking Americans and their credit.

FREDDY ROACH
But,...

WET~RICE
THE INTERNET killed the whole Russian army in one afternoon while tweeting about it. How on flat earth are you going to kill someone as powerful as he is.

FREDDY ROACH
And why are you telling me this?

WET~RICE
Because you are too stupid to realize. If you have anemia and a family that you have no memories of will die unless you kill the most powerful man on flat earth?
    (shaking her head)
You sure are stupider than stupid.

FLASHBACK - THE INTERNET

THE INTERNET, holding a mac-ten machine gun, kills the whole ARMY OF EL SALVADOR.

WET~RICE (V.O.)
He's gangster. The only person that I know that can kill a whole army while still making that country feed him. It's taking your bitch to a whole new level.

Freddy Roach points at the sky.

FREDDY ROACH
You see that?

WET~RICE
That's not a shooting star Professor.

Freddy points toward the shooting star that is heading directly toward them.

> FREDDY ROACH
> Did you wish this?

INT. SIKORSKY X6 - MOVING - NIGHT

> CANTGETRITE
> I do not wish to crash!

> NBA SUPERSTAR
> Fuck off, get on the app, give me a good review!

> CANTGETRITE
> We're going to crash!

> NBA SUPERSTAR
> Not again!

> caNTGETRITE
> Again?
> (beat)
> DaFuck?

EXT. SKY - NIGHT

SIKORSKY HELICOPTER is heading for a crash.

VORTEX OPENS

SIKORSKY HELICOPTER flies into the VORTEX

CantGetRite flies out of the VORTEX without a helicopter

VORTEX CLOSES

INT. PENTAGON - DAY

          POTUS ICE CREAM
My team has located Freddy Roach, and we will be arresting him tonight at his apartment along with CantGetRite.

          THE INTERNET
CantGetRite is the man hired to kill me?

THE DEVIL APPEARS.

          THE DEVIL
Not just him.

          THE INTERNET
Devil!

          THE DEVIL
Net!

          THE INTERNET
I should have known you were behind all this.

          THE DEVIL
Well you want to be a GOD don't you?
     (sarcasm)
I'm a GOD... I'm a GOD... I'm a GOD!

          THE INTERNET
What's your point?

          THE DEVIL
This are just test. Remember? or as it too much data for your little peon conductor of a brain.

> THE INTERNET
> You're always kind enough to remind me.

> THE DEVIL
> And remind I will.
> (Beat)
> Just like your essay. With GOD like powers. They aren't easily given away to. You dumb fuck!

> GOD (O.S.)
> (coughing)
> Bullshit!

A CAT appears.

THE INTERNET grabs the CAT.

> THE INTERNET
> Sure.

> SUPREME CHINA LEADER
> If you promise to release the files of the planet strip.

> MEXICA PRESIDENT
> We promise not to kill you.

> THE INTERNET
> Arrest both and make it public.

> SUPREME CHINA LEADER
> What about all the files The Cockroach has on you?

> THE INTERNET
> I'll delete it all off the servers personally!

> MEXICA PRESIDENT
> How long will that take?

                    THE INTERNET
                (opens and closes his eyes)
        Done.

                    THE INTERNET
        I am a GOD!

                    THE DEVIL
        Relax buddy!

THE INTERNET walks towards the window and throws the CAT out the window.

FLOOR 33

YOU'RE BLACK?

EXT. FREDDY'S APARTMENT ROOFTOP - NIGHT

THE DEVIL, GOD, ALLAH, ODIN, and L. RON HUBBARD all appear as FLIES sitting on the trash can watching.

CANTGETRITE CRASHES INTO FREDDY ROACH.

> ALLAH
> This is like watching live theater.

> GOD
> Shhhh!

BUDDHA appears as a BUTTERFLY.

> ODIN
> Glad you can make it, Bub!

> THE DEVIL
> Fuckin' fairy!

Freddy pushes CantGetRite off of him while noticing his Driver's License in his hands.

> WET~RICE
> You're Black?

CantGetRite gives WET~RICE the side eye while dusting himself off, puts his Driver's License back in his wallet, and looks around in amazement.

> CANTGETRITE
> So this is NEWER OAK CITY.

WET~RICE attempts to touch CantGetRite's hair.

> **WET~RICE**
> Can I touch your hair?

CantGetRite pulls back in confusion.

> **CANTGETRITE**
> Da Fuck.

All the buildings are not taller than 6 floors, and to the East of CantGetRite are the only two buildings on the planet strip to tower over everything.

> **CANTGETRITE**
> Dang!

CantGetRite pulls out his vape pen and shakes it.

> **CANTGETRITE (V.O.)**
> Fuck… running low.

CantGetRite smokes his vape pen.

> **FREDDY ROACH**
> You're Black!

> **CANTGETRITE**
> No shit! Safe to say that both of you aren't blind.

Freddy Roach starts touching CantGetRite's face.

CantGetRite pushes Freddy Roach off of him.

> **CANTGETRITE**
> Seriously what the hell!

WET~RICE trys to touch CantGetRite once more.

CANTGETRITE
I'm not here looking for trouble.

WET~RICE
(stares at CantGetRite's face)
Why you black?

FREDDY ROACH
She means... why are you here?

Freddy Roach and WET~RICE's phone dings a notification from BITCOIN.

BITCOIN (V.O.)
Congratulations! You just earned one BITCOIN!

WET~RICE and Freddy Roach walk around CantGetRite in amazement, making CantGetRite feel like a side showfreak.

CANTGETRITE
What are you guys doing?

WET~RICE
We celebrate. We just got one BITCOIN.

CANTGETRITE
What's your name?

FREDDY ROACH
What's your name?

WET~RICE touches CantGetRice's Afro.

WET~RICE
Is that real?

CantGetRite flinches.

CANTGETRITE
Ok, stop! You guys are making me feel uncomfortable.

FREDDY ROACH
If you tell us who you are.

WET~RICE
We will tell you who we are.

CANTGETRITE
If you two can stop touching me and dancing around me.
    (beat)
I'll answer.

Freddy Roach and WET~RICE continue to skip around CantGetRite.

FREDDY ROACH
Let me guess. Elvis?

WET~RICE
You look like a Ryan.

FREDDY ROACH
Robert?

WET~RICE
Pedro?

CANTGETRITE
I'm not Mexican. I'm black!

FREDDY ROACH
Jo Jackson!

WET~RICE
Jimmy Johnson.

CANTGETRITE
Stop!

WET~RICE
LeRoy!

Freddy Roach and WET~RICE's phone dings a notification from BITCOIN.

BITCOIN (V.O.)
BITCOIN has been successfully deposited.

Freddy Roach and WET~RICE, stop skipping around CantGetRite.

CANTGETRITE
My name is CantGetRite!

FLOOR 34

WORTHLESS 6 MILLION DOLLAR CHECK

CantGetRite looks at his watch and noticed that it's been damaged in the crash.

                CANTGETRITE (V.O.)
      Fucking people these days!

CantGetRite takes off his watch and throws it in the trash.

                L. RON HUBBARD
      That's a nice watch.

                BUDDHA
      Wasteful.

CantGetRite pulls out his cell phone and starts searching for Freddy Roach.

                CANTGETRITE
      I have to get going.

CantGetRite walks away while scrolling through his cell phone.

                WET~RICE
      I'm WET~RICE.

                CANTGETRITE
      Don't care!

CantGetRite climbs onto the ladder and waves goodbye.

FREDDY ROACH
(waving at CantGetRite)
I'm Freddy!

CantGetRite pops his head up.

CANTGETRITE
Last name?

FREDDY ROACH
Roach.

CantGetRite climbs back onto the rooftop and walks towards Freddy with his arms extended.

CANTGETRITE
My muthafucka! Been looking all over for you!

CantGetRite hugs Freddy.

CANTGETRITE
I have check and a message from your father.

FREDDY ROACH
Check?

CantGetRite pulls out a $600,000 check from Ramon Ramon Inc.

Wet~Rice and Freddy grab the check and start staring at it in amazement.

CANTGETRITE
I couldn't believe it myself either!

Freddy Roach starts tearing the check into multiple pieces.

CANTGETRITE
No. No. No. No. No. No!

Freddy Roach tosses the confetti check in the air.

CANTGETRITE
Are you retarded? Please tell me you're retarded!

FREDDY ROACH
I'm Freddy.

CantGetRite drops to his knees to pick up all the ripped pieces.

CANTGETRITE
Your father was right... You're not the smartest egg.

FREDDY ROACH
And how do you suggest I cash it?

CANTGETRITE
There's a thing called.
    (beat)
Banks.

FREDDY ROACH
I don't even remember who my father was!

WET~RICE
It's ok... I'll help you.

FREDDY ROACH
You keep saying that.

CANTGETRITE
Listen... I need you to take this to where ever they cash checks.

WET~RICE
You're not from around here are you?
(off of CantGetRite)
No bank but, we do have BITCOIN!

CANTGETRITE
No banks? No cash. No ATMS?

Freddy and WET~RICE nod NO in unison.

CANTGETRITE
Coins?

Freddy and WET~RICE nod NO in unison.

CANTGETRITE
How do you guys get paid?

FREDDY ROACH
Nope nope nope

CANTGETRITE
What the fuck? Something just doesn't feel right!

FREDDY ROACH
I had the same feeling for years!

THE DEVIL, ALLAH and ODIN fly towards the TRASH CAN.

ODIN
Such a cool ass watch.

ALLAH
It's a Rolex!

THE DEVIL takes one quick look.

THE DEVIL
It's a fake.

FLOOR 35

DEBBIE DOWNER

INT. GOVERNMENT POLICE CAR - NIGHT

A CAT jumps on the Government Police Officer's lap.

Karen and Government Police 310 Officer are heavily making out.

KAREN'S CELL PHONE RINGS

Karen responds to her text message.

     GOVERNMENT OFFICER
  Stop looking at your phone.

     KAREN
  Oh, Officer, you're definably growing a pair.

KAREN'S CELLPHONE RINGS.

Karen responds to her text message.

KAREN'S CELL PHONE RINGS

Government Officer grabs Karen's phone.

KAREN'S CELL PHONE

Multiple text messages from DEBBIE DOWNER with the same message: "Don't stay up too late or we'll be late!"

With multiple responses from Karen: Relax.

Government Officer unzips his pants, takes a photo of his dick, and text it to Debbie Downer.

                GOVERNMENT OFFICER
        She won't be responding back anytime soon.

The CAT jumps out the window.

                    DEBBIE (V.O.)
            You and your kitty. I swear!

FLOOR 36

T.A.P. FOR WORK

INT. FREDDY'S APARTMENT - NIGHT

CantGetRite walks in, jumps on Freddy's sofa, grabs the remote control and turns on the television.

CANTGETRITE LOOKS AT THE CAMERA

> CANTGETRITE
> I'm guessing you are wondering why I look so relaxed. Even after seeing a $600,000 check being ripped in front of me. Defiantly a first for me.

FLASHBACK

EXT. FREDDY'S APARTMENT - NIGHT

> FREDDY ROACH
> THE INTERNET and The Government took away the monetary systems decades ago after the AFTER SHOW. We are all born into debt now and have no way out other than death. They call it the AFTER SHOW.

CantGetRite is trying to tape the check back into one piece with BLACK TAPE and is failing miserably!

> CANTGETRITE
> So you all get paid the same, and no matter what you do, you're in debt? And BITCOIN? What gives?

FREDDY ROACH
Yes, there's no reason to work hard. Unless you are on a work crime debt job, mining Cobalt and no one wants that job. BITCOIN is our Government's assistances.

WET~RICE
Nothing innovative is being made since the AFTER SHOW.

CANTGETRITE
Government-paid boarding? AFTERSHOW? BITCOIN?

WET~RICE
Yes. Yes. And yes!

CANTGETRITE
Are you all working remote?

WET~RICE
Yes. All the best doctors do surgery remote.

CANTGETRITE
Government-paid food?

FREDDY ROACH
Yes.

CANTGETRITE
All you have to do is work?

FREDDY ROACH
Yes.

CANTGETRITE
Slaves to labor-intensive and grueling work from dusk to dawn in an unsafe dirty pit.
(beat)
Right?

FLASHBACK - FREDDY ROACH

EXT. FEDERAL COBALT MINING FACILITY

MOSES
(towards Freddy Roach)
Welcome to the end of your rope. Get use to your surrounds as you will not leave here alive.

Freddy Roach notices a HUGE FINGER appearing out the of sky and killing a MINOR that was running.

MOSES
No one leaves this place alive.

BACK TO SCENE

WET~RICE, shaking her head, as she pulls out her cell phone and shows it to CantGetRite.

CANTGETRITE'S - POV

WET~RICE'S cell phone showing a QR CODE.

CantGetRite scans the QR CODE.

CANTGETRITE'S CELLPHONE

SIRI appears on the THE SCREEN.

T.A.P. APP

> SIRI
> Well, look at you. I'm proud of you! Proud that you decided to take the leap and join in with your fellow Americans in T.A.P. for work. Government work for the great American worker. Proud to be working.

3 JOB IMAGES APPEAR on screen.

> SIRI
> We have 3 different jobs and you can choose from one or all three. It's all up to you. Choices, choices, choices. If you can't decide, feel free to do them all. Freedom at your fingertips! Only from T.A.P.S. The Government on your finger.

> CANTGETRITE
> That doesn't sound like a bad deal at all.

INT. FREDDY APARTMENT - CONTINUOUS

> WET~RICE
> The app is so addicting.

CantGetRite is playing "THE FINGER GAME" on his cellphone.

> CANTGETRITE
> This isn't so bad.

FREDDY ROACH - FLASHBACK

Freddy runs towards a motorcycle while singing to himself.

FREDDY ROACH
(singing)
You ain't fingering me!

Freddy dodges multiple fingers going 60 mph on the street and heading towards the Freeway.

Freddy Roach turns on the RADIO

DJ JILL.MP3 (V.O.)
Welcome back to DJ JILL.MP3. Rocking the music from Universe to Universe.

Freddy jumps onto one of the fingers, lands on top of the Freeway, slams on the gas and goes 100-mph down the freeway

DJ JILL.MP3 can be heard mixing sounds.

INT. FREDDY ROACH'S APARTMENT - NIGHT

CANTGETRITE LOOKS AT THE CAMERA.

CANTGETRITE
I mean you work a little bit.

CantGetRite pulls out his cell phone.

CANTGETRITE
Not like you are being lazy. Just work just enough to also get assistance. Boy, was I wrong! I'm starting to not make sense. Yeah, I admit seeing that check being destroyed affected me in ways I never thought possible.
(takes a long breath)
Fuck...I need a smoke.

BACK TO SCENE

FLOOR 37

HARD PILL TO SHALLOW

          CANTGETRITE
I wonder what's on the tube. Do you know where we can buy some weed and pizza?

          DEVIL (O.S.)
Wait for it.

          FREDDY ROACH
What's weed?

          CANTGETRITE
huh?

          DEVIL (O.S.)
Wait for it!

          FREDDY ROACH
Weed?

          L. RON HUBBARD (O.S.)
Oh, the plot thickens!

          CANTGETRITE
Weed. Pot. Reefer. Grass. Dope. Ganja. Mary Jane. Hash.

Freddy and WET~RICE look confused.

          CANTGETRITE
You know... the good stuff!

          WET~RICE
Rice?

Freddy just shakes his head.

> **CANTGETRITE**
> Oh god no! Please don't fuck with me. You're telling me there's no weed or pizza in this world?

> **WET~RICE**
> Nope. Pizza, yes.

WET~RICE takes out a pill labeled "PIZZA" and hands it to CantGetRite.

> **CANTGETRITE**
> What the fuck is this shit?

> **FREDDY ROACH**
> Pizza. Good O'fashion Government cheese pizza.

CantGetRite pulls out the satellite phone and starts dialing.

> **CANTGETRITE**
> Oh, hell Nah!

FLOOR 38

CALLING THE GODS

INT. UNIVERSE - UNKNOWN

GOD, DEVIL, ALLAH, ODIN, BUDDHA, and L. RON HUBBARD appear

          THE DEVIL
Hello Cant...you rang?

          CANTGETRITE
Rang? Listen you muthafu...what the...
    (looks around)
Who the fuck?

THE CAMERA PANS AROUND CANTGETRITE

          ALLAH
I think it's time that we introduced ourselves to the boy.

          CANTGETRITE (O.S.)
    (Whispers to himself)
Boy?

          GOD
GOD.

          ODIN
Odin

          ALLAH
Allah, the one and only.

BUDDHA
Buddha.

THE DEVIL
The guy on the laptop is L. Ron Hubbard.

L. Ron Hubbard stops typing and waves.

DEVIL
And you already met me. The good-looking of the bunch. The Devil in disguise. Remember my name, you'll be screaming it later. Oh, and the guy on the laptop over there
(Points at L.Ron Hubbard)
Is L.Ron Hubbard.

L. Ron Hubbard stops typing and finger-shoots.

ODIN
Quit messing with the kid.

CANTGETRITE
What in the cotton-picking minute is going on? I did not sign up for this!

CantGetRite does a double take, looking at every single GOD.

CANTGETRITE
Wait... What!

ALLAH
You did.

CANTGETRITE
The fuck I did!

ODIN snaps his fingers

A screen shows CantGetRite, an obviously altered playback video of CantGetRite, agreeing to the contract.

                    BUDDHA
        I would say that you signed under duress.

CantGetRite gives BUDDHA the side-eye while pointing at

                    BUDDHA
              (returning the side-eye)
        BUDDHA.

                    GOD
        I think the kid hit his head.

                    ALLAH
        He looks fine to me.

                    CANTGETRITE
        Ok... who the fuck are you guys again?

                    ODIN
        Jesus Christ... it takes a man to fix this. L.RON,
        Throw up a spread sheet.

L.RON Clicks on the computer.

VIDEO

All the GODS are introduce in the style of the SUPER BOWL.

CantGetRite shakes his head.

ALLAH
(whispers to ODIN)
You do know your black people.

ODIN winks back at ALLAH while finger shooting L.RON who clicks on his keyboard again.

VIDEO ENDS

CANTGETRITE
Hold on hold on now...I'm starting to realize this is all bullshit. Whoever is in fucking control and I know you can hear me you motherfucker! I need to talk to you. Your fucking face to face and you best be one hundred with me bitch!

ALLAH
Wait...

CANTGETRITE
Wait? You ain't in control... there's six GODS.
(mumbles to himself)
How the fuck did you become a GOD.
(clears his throat)
So, Mr. ALLAH. I want to talk to the main man.

FADE TO WHITE

INT. THE UNIVERSE COURT - UNKNOWN

CantGetRite appears to be the plaintiff and THE DEVIL is the defendant.

We do not see THE UNIVERSE, THE UNIVERSE is all around everyone.

> THE DEVIL
> My Universe, CantGetRite cannot, has not, and does not want to fulfill his obligations to the promises at hand, he failed to succeed, meaning he must die and die he...

> THE UNIVERSE
> Mr. CantGetRite. Did you promise to kill the Internet? And did you sign anything with the express knowledge.

> CANTGETRITE
> THE UNIVERSE?

> THE UNIVERSE
> Answer the question Mr. Rite.

MARCUS AURELIUS, 58, Stoic lawyer appears.

> MARCUS AURELIUS
> Your honor your Universe my Universe I need two minutes with my client please.

And in a split second, all sizes of CATS start to appear.

> THE UNIVERSE
> Karen show yourself!

More CATS appear.

> THE UNIVERSE
> Karen!

A HUGE TIGER appears.

THE UNIVERSE SIGHS as Karen appears and looks around in complete confusion.

> **KAREN**
> Where the fuck is mine and how come I wasn't here first fucking class...

Karen stops and looks around.

Karen sees THE DEVIL.

> **KAREN**
> How dare you send me to this wretched piece of shit...

> **THE DEVIL**
> Relax... relax.

> **MARCUS AURELIUS**
> I suggest an injunction sector 76RA on Karen, The Complainer INC., and due to the sector 444 – a also it's in junction connected to the RickoGod 22 Act and may I remind that she just recently got her GOD like abilities.

> **THE UNIVERSE**
> You don't need to remind me of nothing but I grant your request well played you are worth every penny

> **CANTGETRITE**
> What do you mean worth every penny I can't afford to pay you... And that woman is a GOD?

> **THE UNIVERSE**
> Only way I can place an injunction is with at least one GOD to agree with your testimony. Do you have a...

L. RON HUBBARD appears.

                    L. RON HUBBARD
I attest to Marcus Aurelius.

                    MARCUS AURELIUS
Thank you Mr. Hubbard.

MARCUS and L. RON fist bump.

                    L. RON HUBBARD
              (looking at THE DEVIL)
It's my pleasure.
              (beat)
I may be the only GOD that the kitty affects but, I do make notes on the situation.

L. RON HUBBARD pulls out his notebook.

                    L. RON HUBBARD
My Universe. I present you the times and location where the powers were misused.

L. RON HUBBARD'S NOTEBOOK disappears.

                    THE UNIVERSE
              (towards Karen)
I hear by relinquish your God like abilities Karen, you are a disgrace for abusing ability that could've helped you, but more or less you used it for selfish goods, you will no longer be able to complain and get what you deserve.

                          GOD
Typical woman. All that power...

                         ALLAH
And no responsibilities.

BUDDHA
Don't be sexist.

THE DEVIL
Shut up fuck fat face.

KAREN
When I get home, I'm going to file a complaint with your manager and I'm going to...

Karen disappears

THE UNIVERSE
Manger? Karen is on a whole level of stupid and unfortunately for you, Mr. Aurelius, the frequencies are aligning with The Devil.

THE DEVIL
Yes! I win motherfucker.

THE UNIVERSE
But...

THE DEVIL
Oh great the fucking butt.

THE UNIVERSE
Cant, do you understand the reason why?

CANTGETRITE
I didn't promise shit!

THE UNIVERSE
Your word is your bond.

MARCUS AURELIUS
(whispers in Cant's ear)
Stop being emotional.

THE UNIVERSE
Your word is your bond Mr. Rite. It's the only contract that can not be broken. It doesn't matter where. The only thing that matters is the who. The who did give the word. I will Grant injunction and you are extended a whole second.

CANTGETRITE
A second? A whole fucking second?

MARCUS AURELIUS
(whispers in Can't ear)
Calm down.

MARCUS looks dead at CantGetRite's eyes.

MARCUS AURELIUS
(mouthing the words)
Shut the fuck up!

CantGetRite stops talking and composes himself.

MARCUS AURELIUS
I need a moment with my client

THE UNIVERSE
Two minutes. No more. No less.

Marcus and CantGetRite disappear.

INT. MARCUS AURELIUS OFFICE - UNKNOWN

A 90-YEAR-OLD SECRETARY hands Marcus a thick file labeled "CANTGETRITE" while handing CantGetRite a coffee drink.

90-YEAR-OLD SECRETARY
And a mocha, Frappuccino, cookies and cream with whip cream.

CANTGETRITE
How did you know?

CantGetRite continues to look around in ah as he drinks his Frappuccino.

90-YEAR-OLD SECRETARY
You been ordering the same thing for decades.

The 90-YEAR-OLD SECRETARY comes closer to CantGetRite's face.

CANTGETRITE'S POV

A very old looking Woman's face comes close to CantGetRite, startling him.

BACK TO SCENE

90-YEAR-OLD SECRETARY
(towards Marcus)
Same billable address for Mr. Rite?

MARCUS AURELIUS
Yes.

90-YEAR-OLD SECRETARY walks out the door.

Marcus opens up the CANTGETRITE FILE.

CANTGETRITE
She doesn't need to be working.

MARCUS AURELIUS
We been through this.

CANTGETRITE
No. We have not.

MARCUS AURELIUS
She's doesn't like wearing make-up.

CANTGETRITE
She needs to reconsider.

MARCUS AURELIUS
You gave your word that you're gonna kill the Internet yet you did not.

CANTGETRITE
I don't remember.

MARCUS AURELIUS.
It doesn't matter because you are on record and you left The Universe.

CANTGETRITE
I didn't leave shit I can't even afford to go to Florida

MARCUS AURELIUS
Learn to control your emotions. We talked about this.

CANTGETRITE
Control? I just saw six GODS and THE UNIVERSE? Control doesn't seem like a good fit. And. No. We. Have not.

MARCUS AURELIUS
Let me break it down to you so that you can better understand the situation without being overly dramatic.

CANTGETRITE
(mouthing to himself)
Sure.

MARCUS AURELIUS
Or silly.

CANTGETRITE
Ok. Ok. Ok. Ok.

MARCUS AURELIUS
There are 6 billion CantGetRite in 6 billion universes

CANTGETRITE
I thought the universes were unlimited infinite. What do you call it Unknown and all that shit...

MARCUS AURELIUS
It is but I'm putting numbers so you can easily digest and...

CANTGETRITE
It just doesn't sound...

MARCUS AURELIUS
I have two minutes with you so please hold the questions till the end.

CANTGETRITE
Ok. Hit me with it.

MARCUS AURELIUS
One of you. Your crew. You basically. Because there are 6 billion of you. Well one of you decided to leave their universe.

CANTGETRITE
Sounds like I'm a smart muthafucker.

MARCUS AURELIUS
Whatever decision comes consequences, no matter if it's rain or shine there's always an affect to your cause.

MARCUS AURELIUS - FLASHBACK

There's a video of the US PRESIDENT MOND entering the spaceship with the Vietnamese Alien.

MARCUS AURELIUS
(Pointing at MOND)
That is you on a different universe

CANTGETRITE
I'm a president?

MARCUS AURELIUS
Yes.

CANTGETRITE
That's a US president is Latino, do I look Latino to you!

MARCUS AURELIUS
Once again, you're not understanding. I'll resimplify it.

Marcus takes a visible breath.

                    MARCUS AURELIUS (V.O.)
Good!
    (beat)
Good.

                    MARCUS AURELIUS

        It down to you. There are six billion of
        you, one left. It's unbalanced now,
        there's only one CantGetRite in the
        Universe that won. You are going to
        have to unbalanced the universe so
        unfortunately, the only way to make
        balance is for you to kill the Internet in
        another universe.

                    CANTGETRITE
In another Universe?

                    MARCUS AURELIUS
Yes... you are in the Universe were the CantGetRite
left.

                    CANTGETRITE
How?

                                    BACK TO SCENE

Marcus pulls out a remote control and out comes a
COMPUTER SCREEN.

                    MARCUS AURELIUS
Knowitall, brief me on President Mond and the
AFTER PARTY.

SERIES OF SHOTS

A) Aliens land on American soil.

B) US PRESIDENT MOND meets THE ALIEN GROUP

C) US PRESIDENT MOND jumps into the ship with The VIETNAMESE ALIEN.

D) The sonic blast from the space ship slices 80% of the Earth.

BACK TO SCENE

CANTGETRITE
So, I take it, that it's not as easy as cutting the wires like in the movies?

MARCUS AURELIUS
No, in this universe, the Internet is a real threat, and you need to start learning how to defend yourself if you want to survive. After this conversation, you'll be sent back to your universe, where you'll need to convince everyone to take action against the Internet. You'll be transported without anyone here knowing about our discussion.

CANTGETRITE
That's where I'm confused. My mama always told me

THE UNIVERSE (V.O.)

Time.

INT. THE UNIVERSE COURT - UNKNOWN

CantGetRite appears to be the plaintiff and THE DEVIL is the defendant.

THE UNIVERSE
Judgement is death.

THE DEVIL
(to himself)
Yes!

MARCUS AURELIUS
My Universe... How about sector J91 page 4956.

THE UNIVERSE
I see.

CANTGETRITE
See what?

THE DEVIL
Sector J91?

MARCUS AURELIUS
(towards CantGetRite)
Breath!

THE UNIVERSE
Granted!

THE DEVIL
What do you mean granted?

THE UNIVERSE
It means Mr. Devil that Mr. Rite has another opportunity to fulfill your request to balance out the Universe of all the CantGetRite's in the universe and I'm going to grant him the memory to recall all of this. He's not gonna have amnesia like your last plaintive CantGetRite.

THE DEVIL
No!

THE UNIVERSE
No?

THE DEVIL
I mean...now?

THE UNIVERSE
You are held in contempt of the Universe and be sent to HELL.

THE DEVIL
Fuck! Again?

THE DEVIL disappears.

CANTGETRITE
What does this mean?

THE UNIVERSE
Kill THE INTERNET or be wiped off the face of existence.

CANTGETRITE
I'm confused.

MARCUS AURELIUS
Kill THE INTERNET or be killed.

CANTGETRITE
Wha...

CantGetRite disappears.

INT. HELL - UNKNOWN

THE DEVIL appears and sees a sign that reads, " You are at the lowest point of HELL. WELCOME!"

THE DEVIL pulls out his cellphone and quickly notices there's no signal and starts walking around.

                    THE DEVIL
  Fuck!

The Devil approached a flaming pole adorned with an advertisement.

ADVERTISEMENT

ATTEND THE ONE NIGHT EVENT IN HELL with DJ. JILL.MP3 and THE ALIENS on their all over the UNIVERSE TOUR.

THE DEVIL grabs the advertisement.

                    THE DEVIL
       Wow... good quality paper!

FLOOR 39

GRACE OF GOD

GRACE, with short hair, wearing a business dress that fills her beautiful curves while wearing stilettos, walks past ALLAH, ODIN, BUDDHA, L.RON HUBBARD and straight to GOD.

Grace pulls out her tablet.

> GRACE
> I need you to sign here... You're getting way too many requests, and we need to stop them.

> ALLAH
> You know. You're the only GOD I know that has his own personal assistance.

> GOD
> Did you want one? Grace has been with me since the beginning. I'll give you Jemina's Temps. Fantastic customer service from a small business! Love her!

GOD looks at Grace.

> GOD
> You've been a blessing to me.

> GRACE
> That's nice. Sign here.

CU - GRACE'S TABLET

ONE NEW REQUEST FROM CANTGETRITE

THE TABLET auto scans GOD'S face and auto opens CANTGETRITE'S REQUEST

VIDEO

SUPER: TIME STAMP 6 SECONDS - IMPORTANT LEVEL: 0

CantGetRite extends his hands slightly toward the sky.

      CANTGETRITE
    (under his breath)
  Oh God, help me!

SUPER: REQUEST READ. THE DECISION IS BEING PROCESSED.

            END OF VIDEO

      GOD (O.S.)
Deny.

            BACK TO SCENE

      BUDDHA (O.S.)
Oh no.

GOD looking at the tablet.

      GOD
    (mocking CantGetRite)
  Oh God help me?
    (beat)
  You're an atheist man!

      ALLAH
I understand the level of frustration of being overstressed with too many requests.

GOD
How do you deal with it?

ALLAH
They praise me, Allah. They don't beg, which makes it easier. Praise be me, Allah.

GRACE
It's because you don't have a secretary, Allah.

GRACE
Call her. She an hook you up.

FLOOR 40

The Secretary

> **JEMIMA RITE**
> Welcome to Jemima's temp agency. What brings you to my office?

ALLAH gives Jemima

> **ALLAH**
> I was told that you are the best, and I'm seeking a secretary for my needs, but there is one request that has to be met.

> **JEMIMA RITE**
> Let me guess. You want a Muslin.

> **ALLAH**
> That is correct.

> **JEMIMA RITE**
> My top guy won't be available til next week. You are more than welcome to interview him. I believe his is the man that can help you with all your needs.

> **ALLAH**
> Praise be to me.

> **JEMIMA RITE**
> His name is...

FLOOR 41

T-REX

INT. TEXAS PENITENTIARY - DAY

                GUARD
    T-REX step forward!

                T-REX
    How many times do I have to tell you that my name isn't T-REX it's

T-REX, a tall black man with TYRANNOSAURS style arms.

T-REX'S little arms extend to the Guard, barely touching him in the chest.

The Guard looks at T-REX'S arms and laughs.

                GUARD
    You have a visitor.

T-REX picks up the phone through the looking glass where ALLAH sits down and picks up his phone.

                ALLAH
    I was referred to you and was told that you be a great candidate for my corporation.

                T-REX
    What's the position?

                ALLAH
    Assistance or secretary.

                T-REX
    I have experience as you know.

ALLAH
But, before hiring, I like to know a little bit about my employers.

T-REX
Is this an interview?

ALLAH
It can be anything you like. It's your perspective. What is the last book you read, your favorite singer and why are you behind bars?

T-REX
I was arrested on a bogus charge.

ALLAH
Why bogus?

T-REX pulls up his little TYRANNOSAURS style arms.

T-REX
Arrested for assault.

ALLAH
I see.

T-REX
Love Taylor Swift music and my favorite book that I always read is...

T-REX pulls out a miniature KORAN BOOK.

ALLAH
WOW You really are a follower.

T-REX
This book has saved me.

ALLAH
Praise Me.

T-REX
Praise Allah.

ALLAH
I just need a good reference and can you start when you get out?

T-REX
I get out of this joint next week. I do have a great reference.

ALLAH
Great. What's your reference?

T-REX
CantGetRite.

FLOOR 42

ANOTHER CANTGETRITE?

GOD
That can't be CantGetRite?

THE DEVIL
It is, just another Cant in another Universe. What else is fucking new!

ALLAH
I detest jealously.

THE DEVIL
Me? Hahaha. Go bomb a church or something.

GOD
Hey!

L. RON HUBBARD
Not the main one?

THE DEVIL
Nope... I wanna kill him but, he's like a weed. Another Cant will just pop up when you least expected it.

L. RON HUBBARD
I see.

BUDDHA
You can assume.

THE DEVIL
Just for you fat boy. Just for you.

THE DEVIL naps his fingers.

Nothing happens.

THE DEVIL snaps his fingers again.

Nothing happens.

          BUDDHA
Need help little buddy.

          THE DEVIL
Fuck off.

THE DEVIL snaps his fingers.

Nothing happens.

          BUDDHA
Here. Let a fat boy do what an unassuming GOD of fire can't do.

BUDDHA snaps his fingers.

INT. CAR - DAY

SUPER: CANTGETRITE UNIVERSE SECTOR 616.1 - LONG LEGS CANT

          BUDDHA (V.O.)
Not to shabby.

          L. RON HUBBARD (V.O.)
Ok... we are here. Tell us more.

          THE DEVIL (V.O.)
Thank you L. Ron... someone has a brain.

          L. RON HUBBARD (V.O.)
            (mumbling)
Defiantly not you.

          THE DEVIL (V.O.)
See the black man?

          ALLAH (V.O.)
There's two of them.

          GOD (V.O.)
Which one!

          THE DEVIL (V.O.)
The one with the big ass giraffe legs.

LONG LEGS CANT, 6'1, nothing but LEGS sit next to T-REX who is holding the steering wheel with his tiny arms.

          LONG LEGS CANT
Relax... this is a good plan. We be hitting it up tonight.

          T-REX
I'm not so sure.

          LONG LEGS CANT
With my long legs, I be grabbing you outta of there fast and you be the best safe cracker aren't you?

          T-REX
I am.

          LONG LEGS CANT
Can you teach me?

T-REX looks at his tiny hands and looks back at Long Legs.

                    T-REX
Really?

                    LONG LEGS CANT
I be the best cracker that can crack any cracker, you best recognize.

                    T-REX
Lets just get this over with.

                    LONG LEGS CANT
Lets do this.

SERIES OF SHOTS

A) Long Legs Cant grabs T-REX and smashes him into his backpack.

B) Long Legs Cant puts on a ski mask.

C) Long Legs Cant runs into

INT. TEXAS MCKIBBEN BANK - DAY

Long Legs Cant pulls out a hand gun.

                    LONG LEGS CANT
Where's the manager!

                    BANK MANAGER
We want no trouble here son.

                    LONG LEGS CANT
Son!

Long Legs pistol whips the Bank Manager.

     BANK MANAGER
 Please... we have no money here.

     LONG LEGS CANT
 You a bank bitch, now take me to vault.

SERIES OF SHOTS

A) Bank Manager verification ID

     BANK MANAGER
 1,2,3,4,5,6.

B) Bank Manager verification password

     BANK MANAGER
 Big sexy.

C) Bank Manager verification

     LONG LEGS CANT (O.S.)
 Shit man... hurry up!

D) Bank Manager verification sample blood.

E) Bank Manager swaps the blood from his womb onto the verification screen.

F) Bank Manager verification phone 2A

     LONG LEGS CANT (O.S.)
 Fuck man... what's taking so long!

G) Bank Manager's phone bings a verification.

     LONG LEGS CANT
 Hurry up white boy!

BANK MANAGER
Please don't hit me again... I'm going as fast as possible.

LONG LEGS CANT (O.S.)
Not fast enough.

H) Bank Manager verification eye scan.

BANK MANAGER
These new systems where placed yesterday.

I) Bank Manager scan his eyes

J) Bank Manager scans his finger prints.

T-REX (O.S.)
Hurry up!... I can't breathe in this thing!

K) Bank Manager scans his feet.

L) Bank Manager verification voice.

LONG LEGS CANT (O.S.)
Fuck!

M) Bank Manager licks the screen.

VAULT
Success! Welcome to Bank McKibben!

T-REX jumps out of the backpack.

LONG LEGS CANT
Do you magic!

T-REX starts to crack the money vault.

                    T-REX
    Done!

T-REX opens up the vault door.

T-REX AND LONG LEGS CANTGETRITE'S EYES - POV

                    LONG LEGS CANT
    What the fuck!

ONE CRISP DOLLAR BILL

                    T-REX
    DA FUCK!

THE CAMERA ZOOM all through out the bank

BANK ADVERTISEMENT

FREE DONUT FRIDAY FOR ALL COPS

EXT. BANK MCKIBBEN - CONTINUOUS

6 COPS, all with smiles, walk into

INT. BANK MCKIBBEN - CONTINUOUS

                    T-REX
    Lets go.

                    LONG LEGS CANT
    Don't forget the dollar!

                    T-REX
    Lets just go.

LONG LEGS CANT
Grab the dollar.

T-REX
Lets go.

LONG LEGS CANT
Grab the dollar!

T-REX
Its a waste of time.

T-REX grabs the DOLLAR and in walks all 6 COPS.

THE DEVIL
And just like that. 6 years, in 5 minutes. All for just one dollar.

ALLAH
And CantGetRite?

THE DEVIL
He just got assault charges and will be out in a year.

GOD
What about his buddy?

THE DEVIL
Weren't you fucking listening? Or were you too busy with little boys!

BUDDHA
Ok. We got it. He isn't CantGetRite.

THE DEVIL
Fuck fuck fuck fuck... no one listens.

L. RON HUBBARD
(towards ALLAH)
You look like you're in though.

ALLAH
I'm going to hire him as my assistant.

L. RON HUBBARD
Looks to be a winner.

BUDDHA
So is he or isn't a Cant.

THE DEVIL
He is CantGetRite. Just not the core Cant.

BUDDHA
Ah... so everyone is a CANTGETRITE.

THE DEVIL JUST SMASHES HIS HEAD AGAINST THE WALL.

THE DEVIL
No one fucking listens.

THE DEVIL JUST SMASHES HIS HEAD AGAINST THE WALL.

THE DEVIL
No one fucking listens.

THE DEVIL JUST SMASHES HIS HEAD AGAINST THE WALL.

THE DEVIL
No one fucking listens.

Floor 43

Renegotiate

THE DEVIL'S PHONE IS RINGING

> THE DEVIL
> Fuck.

> GOD
> Who is it?

> THE DEVIL
> Fucking Cant

> GOD
> The Cant?

> THE DEVIL
> The Cant.

> L. RON HUBBARD
> Answer it.

ODIN walks in with a box of donuts and a new bank card from BANK MCKIBBEN.

> ODIN
> Praise be these donuts.

> BUDDHA
> Just answer it.

> THE DEVIL
> Who are you my daddy?

> ODIN
> Geez you two.

GOD
Oh me.

Buddha appears in front of GOD.

BUDDHA
Let it go. Let it go.

GOD
Can't hold it back anymore. Ok, you win this one. CantGetRite gets my vote for a renegotiate.

THE DEVIL
The fuck he can. I spent 40 fucking days walking to get out of the dept of HELL because of that retard!

THE PHONE IS RINGING.

THE DEVIL
FUCK!

L. RON HUBBARD
Just answer it and get it over with it.

THE DEVIL
No.

THE PHONE IS STILL RINGING.

THE DEVIL
FUCK!
(answers the phone)
What do you want!

CANTGETRITE
We need to talk.

> THE DEVIL
> Talk bitch.

> CANTGETRITE
> No... in person.

> THE DEVIL
> Fuck you.

> CANTGETRITE
> What are you afraid of bitch!

> ODIN
> Oh I'm liking this guy.

> CANTGETRITE
> Well?

THE DEVIL is about to snap his fingers and just looks at BUDDHA.

BUDDHA snaps his fingers.

CANTGETRITE APPEARS.

> THE DEVIL
> Well look what the trouble brought in. This is all your fault!

> CANTGETRITE
> How was it my fault oh might Devil.

> THE DEVIL
> Well! I'm waiting!

CANTGETRITE looks around and sees all THE GODS staring at him.

> THE DEVIL
> We are all waiting oh great one.

> CANTGETRITE
> I want to renegotiate! I want to go home!

> THE DEVIL
> You want what!

> CANTGETRITE
> I want to renegotiate!

> THE DEVIL
> The fuck you will.

> CANTGETRITE
> The fuck I will.

> THE DEVIL
> Ok smartboy... Kill THE INTERNET, and you can go home!

> CANTGETRITE
> How in the hell does someone kill the internet when the internet is not a dam person?

THE DEVIL'S eyes ponder on CantGetRight.

> THE DEVIL
> You really just asked that question, knowing you are in a room with 6 Gods?

> CANTGETRITE
> Sorry... Yeah, I can see how. You know what... I just shut up.

> THE DEVIL
> It's understandable, but please continue.

> CANTGETRITE
> How in the hell do you kill THE INTERNET?

> GOD
> Sounds like Oh my God! Please help me... Please God, help me. Here's my request. Go fuck yourself!

> ODIN
> Take a chill, GOD... I think someone needs to get laid.

ODIN Looks at Grace's behind as she walks away from sight.

ODIN'S POV

SERIES OF SHOTS

A) Grace walking like she's a supermodel on a catwalk.

B) Grace senses someone staring and looks back directly at ODIN.

C) ODIN and GRACE'S eyes meet.

D) Grace continues to walk til she disappears off THE FRAME.

> ODIN
> I'd love to tap that ass.

> GOD
> Excuse me?

ODIN
I agree with CantGetRite in his negotiate.

THE DEVIL
Trader.

BUDDHA
I second it.

L. RON HUBBARD
Fuck it. This can be interesting. 3rd vote here.

ALLAH
Looks like I can break the debate.

THE DEVIL
What are you going to do about it la la la bomb bomb.

ALLAH
A friend of T-Rex deserves a second chance.

CANTGETRITE
I can go home?

ALLAH
After you kill THE INTERNET.

CANTGETRITE
Fuck!

CantGetRite disappears.

BUDDHA
We got to stop doing this to him.

ODIN
I'm really liking this guy!

FLOOR 44

CANT OR RITE: THE WAGER OF THE GODS

INT. ODIN'S PLACE

ODIN, GOD, THE DEVIL, ALLAH, BUDDHA and L. RON HUBBARD are all sitting on a POKER STYLE TABLE.

THE POKER TABLE is unlike anything in the world.

The Clear table is a WINDOW to all THE UNIVERSES.

Thousands and thousands of UNIVERSES zip across the screen giving it an animated feel.

    DJ JILL.MP3
Ok boy... it's play time.

DJ. JILL.MP3 is the dealer.

    ODIN
I brought everyone together so we can be on common ground and not assume.

    THE DEVIL
So you are thinking the same thing I am?

    ODIN
Yes. What's the wager. Lets discuss.

    BUDDHA
It's good that we are doing this.

    THE DEVIL
Oh shut up.

L. RON HUBBARD
The bet is obvious. Does CantGetRite kill or be killed by THE INTERNET.

ALLAH
Lets keep the bet a mystery and have DJ. JILL.MP3 hold our bets.

L. RON HUBBARD
Well if it's anything like my CantGetRite in my realm... it's going to be an interesting fight.

ALLAH
Agree. What happened to your CantGetRite?

L. RON HUBBARD
He won the California 6 billion dollar lottery and died the next day.

ALLAH
Wow!

ODIN
Was he out of shape?

ALLAH
What happened?

ODIN
I bet he was out of shape.

L. RON HUBBARD
He was in great shape. He just wasn't paying attention to the bus that was headed straight for him when he was crossing the street.

ODIN
Funny because my CantGetRite was in shape. Had a body of a GOD.

L. RON HUBBARD
And what happened to him?

ODIN
He got ran over a train.

GOD
How does that happened?

ODIN
He though he was a GOD. I don't blame him. He had a body of one.

THE DEVIL
Too bad, so sad.

ALLAH
My CantGetRite had the chance to be a track star with his long legs but, the idiot was born in the wrong family.

GOD
Sounds like my CantGetRite.

ALLAH
What about him?

GOD
For some odd fucking reason, this guy watched hours and hours of how to visualization and manifesting that for the life of me. He went out and bought himself a fucking Superman outfit and decided one day that he can fly!

THE DEVIL
Did the poor bastard live?

GOD
That's the surprising factor. Yes! However he's bed ridden for life.

ODIN
Yeah sounds like a Cant. Hey Bub, what about your Cant?

BUDDHA
The kid just died of cancer all of a sudden.

L. RON HUBBARD
Well that's anti-climax. How old was he?

BUDDHA
18. He was the first kid to score a perfect in his SAT SCORES in his Universe.

GOD
Thanks for bring down the vibe with that one. And that leaves us with you DEVIL. Oh that's right you don't have a CantGetRite because your CantGetRite jump into an alien spaceship and left your sorry ass Universe causing us to be in the situation we are. Am I right?

THE DEVIL
What ever!

ALLAH
Well you did find the core CantGetRite.

THE DEVIL
I didn't. Karen was able to find him. Still not sure how the hell, pardon my french. How she found him just blows my mind.

ALLAH
Now that you found him. Are you contempt?

THE DEVIL
Fuck yeah! I can finally see the O.G. CantGetRite die before my eyes but, I love giving people a chance to prove me wrong. Odds are that the O.G. CantGetRite isn't going to last a second with THE INTERNET. Besides this is a fun sport to watch between us. What do you say?

GOD
I think we all can respect that.

ALLAH
So we now know the bet and logistics.

ODIN
What's at stake?

BUDDHA
I see a problem. What if per chance that all of us voted towards CantGetRite and what is the prize?

THE DEVIL
Fat boy is right. Thankfully I'm the genus of the bunch. Lets have six possible winners. Prize number one. First to choose the next GOD.

GOD
(ALLAH)
Please don't elect Taylor Swift.

ALLAH
I love her!

THE DEVIL
Well each of us has fucked up in the way of choices. I fucked up in Karen.
    (looking at Buddha)
See. I can admit when I'm fucking wrong.

BUDDHA
I'm happy for you.

THE DEVIL
No one asked you.

GOD
What's the other prizes?

THE DEVIL
Two second prize would give any one of us the ability take control of another Universe and add it to their collection. Case in point. Taylor Swift Universe that is in my collection. If you picked that. You can steal it from my collection.

ODIN
Oh I'm loving this.

L. RON HUBBARD
Continue. I'm very intrigued.

THE DEVIL
Thank you Ron. And three third prize will be $50 gift card to Red Lobster.

BUDDHA
Yeah.

> THE DEVIL
> That's all she wrote.

> L. RON HUBBARD
> Or did she?

> GOD
> I think it's time we shut the fuck up and we placed our bet.

> ODIN
> Agree with GOD. Minus the shut the fuck up part.

DJ. JILL.MP3 passes out voter cards to everyone.

VOTER CARD READS

WHO WILL DIE? SELECT YOUR KILLER! CANTGETRITE - THE INTERNET

L. RON HUBBARD looks closely at the Voter's Card and can be seen mouthing.

> L. RON HUBBARD
> Who will die? Select your killer? That makes no fuckin'...

> THE DEVIL
> Hurry up Ronny! It's time.

ODIN, THE DEVIL, GOD, ALLAH and BUDDHA have already turned in their voter's card to DJ JILL.MP3.

EVERYONE IS WAITING ON L. RON HUBBARD

L. RON quickly checks the box twice.

THE DEVIL
Just one time buddy... don't need to be so anger with your choices.

L. RON HUBBARD
I guess all bets are in then?

DJ JILL.MP3
Yes.

BUDDHA
(yelling)
UNO!

BUDDHA SLAMS AN UNO CARD DOWN.

All the GODS throw their cards on the table with displeased feeling.

FLOOR 45

I'm learning MA!

> **CANTGETRITE**
> Why me?

> **L. RON HUBBARD**
> You fit the description.

> **CANTGETRITE**
> Oh, how racist of you.

> **L. RON HUBBARD**
> Fuck you!

> **THE DEVIL**
> Oh, loving that passion.

> **CANTGETRITE**
> Well, I didn't sign up for this.

> **BUDDHA**
> Believe you can and believe you have done.

> **THE DEVIL**
> Sounds like you signed up for a tomorrow problem.

THE DEVIL snaps his fingers, and CantGetRite disappears.

> **L. RON HUBBARD**
> You know what. I raise the bet. I'm liking this guy!

> **BUDDHA**
> I'm liking him too.

> **ALLAH**
> So that means you are betting?

BUDDHA
No.

THE DEVIL
Sissy!

GOD
You're on book boy. Buddha, you should join in.

Allah snaps his fingers, and CantGetRite reappears.

CANTGETRITE
What the fuck?

ALLAH
Ok… I will renegotiate for you. Do you agree?

CANTGETRITE
Agree to what? To something much worse? Hell Nah!

ALLAH
No… you'll have a choice. Kill THE INTERNET or survive the next 6 days.

CANTGETRITE
Survive?

Allah snaps his fingers, and CantGetRite disappears.

THE DEVIL
Shit!.. I'm loving this!

CANTGETRITE appears

NO ONE SNAPPED their fingers.

The appearance of CantGetRite astonishes everyone.

CANTGETRITE
Marcus!

Marcus Aurelius appears

MARCUS AURELIUS
I see someone is a fast learner.

CANTGETRITE
Need your assistance. Please.

MARCUS AURELIUS
It's time to renegotiate Boys.

THE DEVIL
There's no negotiating Marcus. The Universe gave it's decision. No love here. It's the Law of the Universe. You should know this.

FLOOR 46

THE DEVIL

THE DEVIL is by himself, sitting on a lawn chair, reading: BE WATER MY FRIEND. THE TEACHINGS OF BRUCE LEE

We PAN OUT to see

INT. FINGER-ME SPA - DAY

BUSINESS POSTER READS: "Get Fingered only at FINGER-ME SPA. The only spa with a finger 24 hours.

Ask about our "TWO FINGER GROUP DISCOUNT!"

THE DEVIL stops reading and notices something as he looks up and down and all around.

THE DEVIL looks straight at the camera.

THE DEVIL looks up and notices that it reads: FLOOR 46: CHAPTER: THE DEVIL

THE DEVIL clicks on the Chapter that is above him which shows a hologram of the book: "

CantGetRite: "To Be Debt-Free, We Must Kill THE INTERNET!"

THE DEVIL, GOD, ALLAH, ODIN, BUDDHA and L. RON HUBBARD walk into a bar……

THE DEVIL, forgetting it's a hologram, falls forward after missing.

THE DEVIL
No fucking way!

THE DEVIL just stares at the hologram as the cover of the book disappears.

THE DEVIL
Oh Mr. UNIVERSE!

THE UNIVERSE APPEARS ALL AROUND.

THE DEVIL
I do not consent or give permission to have my name used. Who the fuck does he think he is?

THE UNIVERSE
He another CantGetRite from another universe.

THE DEVIL
I though CantGetRite was a black thing?

THE UNIVERSE
Don't be a racist prick. Let me remind you that if the core CantGetRite gets Rite, than it will triculate to the other CantGetRite. Giving them hope and...

THE DEVIL
I remember. Winning is contiguous... I get it.

THE UNIVERSE
No. You don't.

THE DEVIL goes back to his chair and continues to Read his book, showing no care.

THE UNIVERSE
I guess you aren't the smartest GOD of them all. If the core CantGetRite. Gets Rite and succeed in Killing THE INTERNET.

THE DEVIL drops his book as his eyes widen in fear.

THE DEVIL
He becomes a GOD.

FLOOR 47

BOOK BURNING

INT. FREDDY'S APARTMENT - NIGHT

CantGetRite wakes up on Freddy's sofa.

CANTGETRITE LOOKS AT THE CAMERA.

> CANTGETRITE
> It has come to my attention that I'm not in my world. I have to survive 6 days or Kill THE INTERNET? Like why would anyone want to kill THE fucking INTERNET? Plus, survive what? Hunger? What the fuck did I do to deserve this shit!

CANTGETRITE'S FLASHBACK

INT. JEMIMA'S HOUSE - NIGHT

SUPER: 38 YEARS AGO - Christmas Eve

Jemima gives a 9 year old CantGetRite, $6.00

> JEMIMA RITE
> Here's $6. Go to the corner store and buy a piece of firewood. It's going to snow. Can you believe it? Jesus has blessed us with snow.

INT. CORNER STORE - NIGHT

> CANTGETRITE
> $9.99 for a piece of wood?

It's starting to snow outside.

> CORNER STORE CLERK (O.S.)
> How the fuck does it snow in CommiCalifornia. Hey kid, either buy something or get the fuck out!

> CANTGETRITE (V.O.)
> Even back in the day, I was very resourceful with money.

CantGetRite grabs a chocolate bar, marshmallow, gram crackers, soda and a Plastic-Man comic book.

> CANTGETRITE (V.O.)
> $6 for a piece of firewood when I can get that shit for free across the street.

SERIES OF SHOTS

A) CantGetRite steals a pack of gum when the Store Clerk isn't looking.

B) CantGetRite walks towards the door exit and stops for a moment.

C) CantGetRite pulls out the stolen gum and leaves it on the countertop near the exit.

D) CantGetRite walks through the exit.

EXT. CHURCH OF SHAW - NIGHT

CantGetRite runs across the street, opens up his backpack, and quickly throws in 5 books from the free library stand outside the Church's double doors.

INT. JEMINA'S HOUSE - NIGHT

                JEMIMA RITE
Start the fire, Cant. When I'm done with my shower, how would you like to have some pancakes for dinner?

CANTGETRITE LOOKS AT THE CAMERA

                CANTGETRITE
First things first, asshole. Stop assuming! First of all, I want you to know that I'm 9 years old! How would I know what I'm doing would cause distress to certain people in higher power who seem to think that the world revolves around them like if they were the Gods of us all and shit.

SERIES OF SHOTS

A) CantGetRite opens up his backpack and pulls out The Koran

                CANTGETRITE
           (Reading the book cover)
The Korean

B) CantGetRite throws THE KORAN in the fireplace.

C) CantGetRite pulls out the Bible.

                CANTGETRITE
           (Reading the book cover)
The Bible.

D) CantGetRite throws THE BIBLE in the fireplace

E) CantGetRite pulls out the book, "BUDDHISM: Living Buddha, Living Christ."

CANTGETRITE
Buddhism.

F) CantGetRite throws the book about BUDDHISM in the fireplace.

G) CantGetRite pulls out the book, "The Mead of Poetry."

CANTGETRITE
The Mead of Poetry.

H) CantGetRite pulls out the book, "Dianetics by L.RON HUBBARD."

I) CantGetRite throws the book, Dianetics, into the fireplace.

J) CantGetRite lights a match and tosses it in the fireplace.

K) All Five Books erupt into a small fire.

L) CantGetRite is roasting marshmallows while reading his comic book.

CANTGETRITE
And how would I know? I'm Cant. I was enjoying the fire. Only wish I didn't.

M) CantGetRite tosses the Comic book, Plastic-Man issue #1

CANTGETRITE
Throw in that comic book. Would have been worth some money right now.

CantGetRite is eating his s'mores while enjoying the fire.

CANTGETRITE
(singing)
On the twelfth day of Christmas, ol' Krampus promised me: Twelve lacerations Eleven bodies burning Ten tar pits boiling Nine inbreds drowning Eight corpses bleeding Seven brains-a-leaking Six sixty six deaths Five organs crushed Four severed limbs, Three blood clots Two eyes-a-gauged And a hung man in a dead tree

JEMIMA RITE (O.S.)
(yelling)
Who taught you this?

CANTGETRITE
(yelling)
Mr. Todd, my English teacher.

BACK TO SCENE

FLOOR 48

PILLS TO SURVIVE

INT. FREDDY ROACH'S APARTMENT - NIGHT

    CANTGETRITE (V.O.)
And here I'm thinking. This world can't be all that bad.

    FREDDY ROACH
A one. A two. A one-two a one two...

    CANTGETRITE (V.O.)
Boy, oh boy, was I dead wrong like all my failed English tests.

    FREDDY ROACH & WET~RICE
Happy Birthday to you. Happy Birthday to you…you look like a monkey, and you smell like one too!

WET~RICE gives CantGetRice

CU- CANTGETRITE'S HAND

Pill reads, "Slice of Vanilla Plan Cake."

CantGetRite looks at Freddy and WET~RICE in confusion.

    FREDDY ROACH
    (off of CantGetRite)
Oh, when you crashed landed on me.

FREDDY'S FLASHBACK

CantGetRite tumbles onto Freddy.

FREDDY ROACH (V.O.)
Not sure why you had your Identification card in your hand when you crashed into me

SMASH CUT TO:

CANTGETRITE'S FLASHBACK

Helicopter nosedived toward the ground.

NBA SUPERSTAR pulls out a credit card reader.

NBA SUPERSTAR
Pay me!

CANTGETRITE
What?

NBA SUPERSTAR
(Pushing the card reader)
Pay me!

CANTGETRITE
We're going to die!

NBA SUPERSTAR
It's all the more reason to get paid!

CantGetRite pulls his CALIFORNIA DRIVER'S LICENSE.

NBA SUPERSTAR
That doesn't look like you left home without it!

The Helicopter crash lands, ejecting CantGetRite out the window and onto Freddy.

The Helicopter disappears along with the fire and wreckage.

Freddy notices

CU - CANTGETRITE'S CALIFORNIA'S DRIVER LICENSE

September 11, 1974

SMASH CUT TO:

INT. FREDDY ROACH'S APARTMENT - NIGHT

                CANTGETRITE
          (hold the pill)
What is this?

                FREDDY ROACH
Nothing but the best Government issued Vanilla cake by the slice.

                CANTGETRITE
No seriously.

WET~RICE grabs the pill, shoves is in CantGetRite's mouth and forces CantGetRite to swallow it.

                WET~RICE
Isn't it the best cake you ever had?

                CANTGETRITE
No!.. That was not even
          (shocked)
Satifilying.

WET~RICE pull down her mask and swallows a pill while Freddy flips one in the air, landing in Freddy's open mouth.

                CANTGETRITE
Ok… What about regular food.

Freddy pulls out his PILL BOX with clearly labeled pills: "ONE DAY NUTRITION ON EACH PILL"

CantGetRite runs into Freddy's

KITCHEN

          CANTGETRITE
Where's the stove?

          FREDDY ROACH
Stove?

          CANTGETRITE
Refrigerator?

          FREDDY ROACH
Only high-level citizens and government officials are allowed to have refrigerators. If you want one so badly, all you have to do is mine Cobalt for the Government.

          WET~RICE
Tell him about candy.

          CANTGETRITE
Candy?

          FREDDY ROACH
Yes, actually, we do have candy.

          CANTGETRITE
Yes! Oh dam. You guys scared me for a bit.

Freddy pulls out another pill.

CantGetRite grabs the pill and looks at the label, "CANDY PILL."

CANTGETRITE
Oh, for fuck sakes!

WET~RICE grabs the pill off of CantGetRite's hand and swallows it.

WET~RICE
Oh yes!

CANTGETRITE
No Alcohol, no food, no weed!?

WET~RICE
The food administration is controlled by the government.

FREDDY ROACH
THE INTERNET controls the Government.

WET~RICE
In turn, there is no...

CANTGETRITE
Food?

WET~RICE
No

CANTGETRITE
Weed?

WET~RICE
No.

CANTGETRITE
Alcohol?

WET~RICE

No.

CANTGETRITE

Nothing?

FREDDY ROACH

Well... I can get you some meth if you are that desperate.

CANTGETRITE LOOKS AT THE CAMERA

CANTGETRITE

This, got to be Hell. Am I in hell?... Cant, you aren't in HELL... going to kill that Devil. Can a GOD be killed? If THE INTERNET is a GOD. Am I fucked? I already feel fucked! Of all the places. A place with no weed.

CU - CANTGETRITE'S EYES

Getting angry.

CANTGETRITE

6 days or be done with it in one. At home, I at least can smoke my life away with some Cheetos and beer to wash my dreams away. No fucking way, this is my end.

THE DEVIL (V.O.)

You signed a contract!

CANTGETRITE LOOKS AT THE CAMERA

CANTGETRITE

Like, what in the fuck is retarded in this bejesus world. Can't I just call customer service and kill the Internet?

ALL THE GODS (V.0)
(Unison)

No!

BACK TO SCENE

INT. FREDDY ROACH'S APARTMENT - CONTINUOUS

CANTGETRITE
We need to kill THE INTERNET!

Freddy and WET~RICE'S eyes widened.

FLOOR 49

ARRESTED

INT. FREDDY'S APARTMENT - CONTINUOUS

DOZENS OF GOVERNMENT POLICE busts into Freddy's Apartment.

> GOV. POLICE #1
> In accordance with section 6 dash 6.6 of THE INTERNET penal code of THE POWER 3A... I hear by place you all under arrest for colluding to take over the Government and attempting to kill THE INTERNET!

> CANTGETRITE
> Oh, come on!

GOV. Police #1 walks up to CantGetRite.

> GOV. POLICE #1
> Papers!

> FREDDY ROACH
> He's with me.

> GOV. POLICE #1
> Shut up, Cockroach!

Freddy's eyes widened.

Freddy and WET~RICE look at each other.

Freddy Roach is being handcuffed while the other Government Police officers raid his apartment.

GOV. POLICE #2 (O.S.)
Found it!

Gov. Police #2 brings Freddy Roach's COCKROACH COSTUME.

GOV. POLICE #1
(on the phone)
We found him!
(beat)
Yes, Sir I will.
(towards Freddy Roach)
Put it on!

THE INTERNET appears in the form of a HOLOGRAM

THE INTERNET
We finally meet.
(beat)
Cockroach.

Freddy Roach, dressed in his full COCKROACH COSTUME.

FREDDY ROACH
INTERNET.

THE INTERNET
Did you not think I would not find you?

CANTGETRITE
Wait... you're THE INTERNET?

THE INTERNET Scans CantGetRite's body.

THE INTERNET
You're not from this strip. Answer me, Ginger! Where are you from!

                    CANTGETRITE
Ginger?

                    GOV. POLICE #1
Shut up Ginger!

                    CANTGETRITE
So you think you're a big badass... why don't you come and say it to my face.

                    THE INTERNET
Oh, you defiantly are not from here. Who sent you?

                    CANTGETRITE
Your bitch ass girlfriend!

THE INTERNET snaps his fingers.

GOV. Police #3 punches CantGetRite in the back of his head.

                                        CUT TO:

FLOOR 50

6 SECOND TRIAL

INT. FEDERAL PRISON DETAINMENT CENTER - NIGHT

CantGetRite wakes up.

                FREDDY ROACH
      Did you really have to insult his girlfriend?

                CANTGETRITE
      Where are we?

GOV. Police #1 opens up the cell.

                GOV. POLICE #1
      Your trial is about to start, Cockroach. You to Ginger!

                CANTGETRITE
      What the hell is with Ginger! I'm...

CantGetRite notices that he is talking to himself while Freddy is pacing the small jail cell.

                CANTGETRITE
      Trial? Again!?

INT. COURT - NIGHT

The court case is being LIVE STREAMED to everyone on the PLANET STRIP.

THE DEVIL is dressed up as the JUDGE.

CANTGETRITE
Ramon Ramon?

THE DEVIL
You will address me, Lord Almighty!

CANTGETRITE
(sarcasm)
Oh Lord!

THE DEVIL
This court finds you guilty on all counts and sentenced you to death by debt!

CantGetRite starts walking towards HUE in handcuffs.

THE DEVIL
Take one more step and...

CANTGETRITE
And what? Charge me for possession as well?

CantGetRite takes off his shoe and throws it at HUE.

CANTGETRITE
Ok, this is becoming an issue!

INT. UNIVERSE

THE DEVIL is dancing while reading the headline news.

THE DEVIL - POV

THE DEVIL'S CELLPHONE

CANTGETRITE FOUND GUILTY: SENTENCED TO DEATH BY DEBT

> THE DEVIL (O.S.)
> Guilty muthafucka... I gots you!
> (beat)
> I finally gots you!

CHESS NOTIFICATION - BING BING

INT. VIETNAMESE ALIEN'S TUNING FORK - UNKNOWN SPACE

US PRESIDENT MOND and VIETNAMESE ALIEN are traveling in light speed through the galaxy.

> US PRESIDENT MOND
> (in Vietnamese)
> I almost forgot.

> VIETNAMESE ALIEN
> Oh babe, yo Vietnamese is getting better. So happy.

US PRESIDENT MOND pulls out his cellphone and clicks the

CHESS APP

CANTGETRITE_CHESS_OVERLORD

A CHESSBOARD opens to a gameplay in process.

Last move: 6.5 YEARS

US PRESIDENT MOND moves the KNIGHT. N3D#

INT. UNIVERSE

THE DEVIL'S CELLPHONE CHESS NOTIFICATION. DING DING.

CHESS APP
Checkmate! CantGetRite wins.

THE DEVIL
Fuck!

THE DEVIL throws his cellphone.

FADE TO BLACK

FLASHBACK - CANTGETRITE

A SERIES OF FLASHBACKS quickly zooms into CantGetRite's mind.

CantGetRite remembers everything.

CLOSE-UP ON CANTGETRITE'S EYES

CANTGETRITE (V.O.)
God dam it!

TO BE CONTINUED……

RAY MOND

Writer - Teacher - Business Owner - Designer - Actor and Traveler

BOOK 2
PART NORTH
COMING SOON

KILL THE INTERNET

Made in the USA
Columbia, SC
26 July 2024

1cb04078-802e-4291-8a9f-9c87fdadb34cR01